TARWA

Myth & Memory

Return of the Dispossessed

An African Journey To The Future

By

Alf E.F. Muronda

ISBN: 978-1-965398-42-5
© Elfigio F Muronda
Published by MASAKA PUBLISHING MEDIA HOUSE
alf@cp7sisters.com

Table of Contents

For My Grandfathers

PRELUDE
King Chokwedu – the Lion

Prince Zharara became the first king of Matonganyika when he led his clan from the valley of the great river in the north, the place where the world begins. The ancestors had ordained him to lead his people from Rimuka, the palatial home of their ancestors, to the land of their future.

To the prince, and to the prince alone, a vision of their future homeland was revealed. Far to the south, the land lay cradled among mountains and scattered hills, looking out over valleys that stretched from the highlands deep in the interior all the way to the eastern ocean. It was a land full of promise. To the west, it was bordered by the lands of the Kaonde people. To the east were the lands of the Makonde, which in turn bordered the lands of the Lomwe. And to the south lay the land of the people of Great Zimbabwe.

Prince Zharara, chosen and guided by the ancestors, brought his people across vast distances to establish their new home. So pleased were the ancestors with his leadership that the Creator blessed him with a long life. By the time he laid down his body to join the ancestors, King Zharara had lived to see his people flourish, his great-great-grandchildren filling the land with their offspring.

Peace and prosperity reigned across Matonganyika for generations. By the tenth generation, their own Rimuka had grown. It had become a sprawling palatial complex of stone and wood cottages, with grass-thatched roofs surrounded by tall, elegant rondavels painted in yellow, brown, and white triangles and circles. Rimuka had no equal, it was the pride of Matonganyika, modeled after their ancestral homeland in the valley of the great river where the world begins.

The people of Matonganyika knew no war. They bore no weapons and held no memory of war. They were hunters, builders, carpenters, traders, farmers, and cattle barons. Their artisan work in gold and copper became renowned far beyond their borders. In times of drought, neighboring kingdoms relied on Matonganyika's granaries. Even in the year of the locusts, when the dreaded *whiza* stripped the rapoko fields and forests bare, Matonganyika had grain to lend until the next harvest.

Strong blood ties through royal marriages, trade, and peace treaties with the Wechinge, Dokari, Tembote, and Pendani, alongside the protective embrace of mountain ranges and the ocean made Matonganyika an idyllic kingdom, shielded from hostile forces by both man and nature.

For generations, Matonganyika basked in peace and prosperity.

However, unfortunately for Matonganyika, there came a generation of elders of the clan and kings who grew complacent. They no longer followed the custom of climbing the sacred hill to attend to the fire of the half-burnt log of the ancestors.

The half-burnt log that Prince Zharara had brought down many generations ago from the valley of the great river in the north where the world begins, had lost its flame. By tradition, the elders and kings would climb the hill and assemble there to deliberate the matters of the day and seek guidance from the ancestors, kindling the flame of the sacred log. But they had forgotten their sacred duty, and the flame had died. Though the half-burnt log itself could not be consumed; without any flame, its power lay dormant.

With no flame to lift their voices skyward, the kings of Matonganyika were unheard. Their ancestors, who once spoke to the Creator on their behalf, now stood in silence.

Matonganyika stood alone, living off the fading glory of the past, the work and prayers of generations long gone. Now, they were on their own.

Chapter One

Unlike his predecessors, King Chokwedu did not have the good fortune to live a long life in the idyllic land of peace and prosperity.

When King Chokwedu ascended to the throne, vaMatinenga who was betrothed to the king at birth, became the queen, the first wife of the king. Like his forefathers, Matonganyika kings before him, he added more dwellings to the royal palace and took in more wives.

King Chokwedu was the image of his royal ancestor, the Great King Zharara. He was a gentle giant; a tall regal black man who dispensed justice with kindness, a fair trader and wise steward of the wealth of his kingdom. His physical stature matched his standing in the eyes of the ancestors and the people of the land. He was hailed "the Lion". He was loved by his people and was admired by their neighbours. By the time of his reign, the people of Matonganyika bloodline lived in villages stretching the distance of a journey that took one full moon to the next full moon. The mountains and valleys overflowed with their livestock: herds of cattle, goats and sheep. Their fields of rapoko, groundnuts and pumpkins were a sight to see.

During all seasons, winter, spring and summer Rimuka was the center of all life for Matonganyika. Each season had its own celebrations. Celebrations for bountiful harvests; prayers for good rain; celebrations of successful transactions with traders; receptions for visiting royalty and emissaries and celebrations and prayers to the ancestors and the Creator for the good health and long life of the king.

By day the center court at Rimuka was a beehive of trading in cloth, jewelry, gold and livestock. By night, under the moon light and torches mounted in the perimeter, centre court became a dance floor where drummers and mbira players entertained the king, his family, courtiers, visiting emissaries, traders and the people from the villages.

Under the easy grace of King Chokwedu, life at Rimuka was an enchanted reverie that became the envy of forces the peaceable king and his people had not prepared for.

In the summer of the year that marked the beginning of the end of Matonganyika, the once-idyllic land of peace and prosperity, emissaries from neighboring allies arrived in Rimuka. The Wechinge, Dokari, Tembote, and Pendani sent their envoys to sit in counsel with King Chokwedu and the elders of Matonganyika.

They brought grave warnings: a plague of ruthless, yellow-bearded men was descending from the north and the ocean. These marauding invaders were armed with dynamite, Gatling guns, and rifles. Wherever they had passed, they left devastation, warriors mowed down, villages reduced to ash, and able-bodied men captured and conscripted as porters.

The invaders respected no king, chief, or headman. No one understood their true purpose, only that they planted flagpoles bearing red, blue, and white cloth, proclaiming that all the land now belonged to their distant king.

King Chokwedu heard the message and began preparing for war, rallying Matonganyika and its allies. Like all kings before him, he knew of the sacred hill where Prince Zharara, the founding father of the clan laid the half-burnt log from the inextinguishable fire of the ancestors. Yet in this desperate hour, he lacked the presence of mind to climb the hill with the elders of the clan to seek the guidance of the ancestors.

King Chokwedu would rue the day he forgot to inform the ancestors of the impending war he had been warned about. The ancestors, who do not interfere in the affairs of men unless invited, sat in silence. Matonganyika and its people were on their own.

It was that time of year when the days counted themselves out with the ripening crops in the fields yearning to be harvested: that time of year when the young boys and girls played games in the unmanned fields; that time of year when grandmothers, with time on their hands, sat down under the shady *msasa* tree away from the hustle of the king's court and told stories of the tricky hare and the gullible baboon to their grandchildren; that time of year when men roasted meat and sweet groundnuts by the fire anticipating a bountiful harvest and thanked the ancestors for the blessings of plenty.

It was during that time in the year that now rests in infamy for Matonganyika, they heard their neighbours in the lands beyond the mountains pound the drums of war. They were sorrowful drums: - dirges that gagged on a plaintive wail of death. The white hurricane had swooped their land as it soon would swoop Matonganyika, King Chokwedu's kingdom.

Their neighbours fell and their wail died with their drums.

War descended upon the land like an errant summer tropical cyclone full of thunder and hailstones. Propelled by a foreign avaricious spirit, the white hurricane eddied over the mountains and set its sights on Matonganyika.

With ferocious relentlessness, the hurricane of Gatling gun and dynamite marshaled European white men into their lives. Disdainfully the hurricane swept away their dance and laughter into the rivers of ages. Their warrior neighbours had marched against the invaders, but their single-action bolt rifles were no match for the white hurricane with its Gatling Guns and dynamite. The white hurricane snapped their shafted spears, bows and arrows like dry reeds and sand pebbles in a volley of harsh winter winds.

Their Africa was no more.

Armed with spears, cow hide shields, musket hunting rifles, and knobkerries but no memory of war, King Chokwedu, the Lion, could only roar exhorting the warrior spirits of old to come to defend the land. His people, like their king, had no memory of war, no weapons to match the marauders and no place to hide.

The white hurricane gathered momentum, burning and looting, leaping and scaling over abandoned fields, over the hills, through all the villages, hamlets, destroying Rimuka. Not a stick nor a stone of Rimuka palatial splendour was left standing. While his clansmen in the outlying villages were able to escape and seek refuge as far away as they could, the rest stayed doing the best they could to defend themselves. King Chokwedu, the Lion, roared and stomped the hard earth leading his people in prayer to the ancestors pleading to be delivered from their fate.

They shouted amid flying bullets, bayonets and dynamite.

Fighting back as best as they could with no weapons to match the enemy, they refused to surrender. On their lips was the vigour of their pride as Matonga shouting, "This is Matonganyika. Rimuka is our home. This land is our birth right! You may win today, but you will not win this war! We are Matonga! Matonganyika is our homeland""

They cried; they would not run and hide.

However, like their neighbours beyond the mountains, they could neither stop dynamite with their tears nor the Gatling gun with their cow-hide shields.

They died as honourably as they could.

Bathed in the blood of the dead men and women of Matonganyika, King Chokwedu looked at the carnage around him. His people, his palace, his land, and his livestock had all been plundered and destroyed. The stench of death and burning grass-thatched roofs filled the air. But he was still alive. He was the last man standing. Hopelessly outnumbered and out maneuvered, he was living on borrowed time. He scooped the remnants of his family, a tattered bunch of old wives and dying young men and young women who had shielded the old people with their bodies and fled to the mountains.

Their reception in the mountains, in refuge, was no less dastardly. The mountains stared at them with indifference as if the spirits of the ancestors had departed in flight ahead of the white hurricane. No king before the Lion, King Chokwedu, had ever suffered such devastation. Thus, without the antecedence of experience, he had not prepared for the calamity. There was no food or shelter in the mountains. If hunger and the harsh weather would not kill them, the beasts of the mountains did.

One by one, he watched the survivors of his people succumb to a hostile world turned to blood and fire bent on their destruction. He entreated and begged the ancestors for a miracle, but no one heard him, and the nightmare grew with each day.

In the solitude of a cave-turned-bunker, where he had led the remnants of his clan to hide, King Chokwedu had a moment of clarity. He was the king who had lost the birthright of his people, the land of Matonganyika. He realized he had tried to fight alone. He had not gone up to the fire of the ancestors, the same ancestors who had birthed them and bequeathed them the land. The half-burnt log of the inextinguishable fire was still out there but it had no flame. Only the living could feed the fire to create flames that showed the ancestors that their guidance was needed. Had there been a fire, the ancestors could have saved them.

But it was too late.

He resolved that the clan would live to fight another day.

Finally, as the true patriarch of Matonganyika, he resolved to preserve the name of Chokwedu and secure the future of his clan's bloodline. He descended from the mountains, bearing what remained of their greatness: an infant boy born to vaMarunjeya, his youngest wife - his only son, born in the wilderness of refuge and hunger.

With the sharp point of his scepter, the royal staff, the king inscribed his mark into the boy's left palm - an indelible symbol of his lineage.

He named the child "Tarwa" denoting that they had done their best, they would live to fight another day.

They came down the mountain to meet their fate.

The king was in front, followed by Chamboko, keeper of his charms and servant-guard, vaMatinenga, his host queen and the junior wives carrying the infant prince and his mother.

They walked into the waiting arms of the white men.

King Chokwedu, the Lion, surrendered and was hung that same morning from a tree as a rebel. When the deed was done, the white men departed, leaving the king's body hanging from the tree.

Chamboko took charge of his master's body amid the grieving, widowed wives who wailed and beat their chests in anguish, decrying their helplessness against the enemy who had hung their king. Chamboko cut down the rope and brought the king's lifeless body down and slung it over his shoulder before it touched the ground. Without speaking, he pointed at the mountain and began walking back up the mountain carrying his master.

In the shuttered bunker where they had found refuge in the mountain, Chamboko laid the king's body down to lie in state.

The dark cloud over Chamboko's heart was the thought of burying his master, King Chokwedu, the Lion of Matonganyika, with a burial unworthy of the great man. His master was royalty, deserving of the sacred rites reserved for Matonganyika kings. But there was nothing he could do. They were far from Rimuka, and for now, the mountainside was all they had. Here, among the stones and silence, Chamboko would lay his master to rest and pray that the great king's spirit would be as compassionate and understanding in death as he had been in life.

The next day, calling to the dead king's spirit to forgive him, shaking his head in despair, Chamboko gingerly picked up the king's body to go down to his eternal resting place. He felt the weight of the king's body as he stumbled his way out of the shattered bunker down to the grave they had dug in an incline in the mountain. As he struggled his way down to the grave where the king's widows waited for him, his mind took inventory of all the missing pieces that tradition held for a royal Matonganyika burial. He was thinking, had they been in Rimuka, a convocation of the spirit mediums and seers of the land would have been assembled to call on the king's ancestors to receive their worthy son in the land of the spirits. From dawn to dusk, the lyrical voices of the griots of the king's court would have serenaded the kingdom reciting the history of Matonganyika and recalling the names of all Matonganyika kings from Prince Zharara to King Chokwedu. His forty five sons and daughters would have led the phalanxes of young Matongas matching throughout the kingdom with the maidens of the land ululating, chanting praises and gratitude to the patriarch for his prodigious accomplishments, his wisdom and the prosperity he had brought upon them all.

Chamboko's reverie was just that, the king's wake was a meager supplication, unworthy of one who had been so large and so generous in life. His widows led by the Queen Mother, vaMatinenga had gathered bundles of tall leafy grass and supple tree branches and made a makeshift altar where Chamboko placed the dead king's body to lie down before they lowered his body into the earth. Their solitary voices and the painful sobs falling from their heavy hearts were all there was to bid farewell to their beloved King of Matonganyika, the doyen of Rimuka. There was no requiem of Matonganyika drums to soothe her sorrow as the Queen Mother nodded to Chamboko to proceed to lift King Chokwedu's body and place it in the grave.

As he lowered the body into the grave, Chamboko, in his role as the king's servant-guard and keeper of his charms, led the king's widows chanting appeals to the king's spirit to forgive them and accept the merger burial ceremony as the best they could do in the mountain of refuge. Chamboko entreated, *"King Chokwedu! Ruler of all Matonganyika! Lion! We remain loyal and exult your great name! Go well my master! Go well Great King! We lay your body here, in this grave, but your spirit forever resides in your palace, Rimuka!"*

vaMatinenga responded: *"Our husband, Father and Master, we know you shall return with more power, with the armies of your ancestors! My Lord we only lost a battle. We know you will not lose the war! You are the Lion, go well to your ancestors".*

Then together, they all sang and chanted *"Go well Great King! Come back Great King! Go well Great King! Come back Great King!"*

Chapter Two

By the will of the ancestors, Chamboko, the king's servant-guard and keeper of his charms, escaped the fate of his master. After the burial of the king, they all continued to mourn the king, but Chamboko's thoughts were on the infant son.

All the late king's wives, including vaMarunjeya, the boy's mother, shaved their heads and pledged a vow of bereavement: to live out the rest of their days beside their husband's grave on the mountain, where they had laid him to rest. However, Chamboko pleaded against such fate for the infant son.

"Queen Mother," Chamboko said softly, choosing his words with care, "for the infant to live here is to bury him too, alongside his father." His words to vaMatinenga, the late king's eldest wife and leader of the royal widows, were all he said.

After days of deliberation, the Queen Mother asked what future awaited the boy in Chamboko's homeland. Chamboko, honest and solemn, admitted he hadn't returned there since childhood, back when he'd visited with his late father, before the white hurricane had swept across Africa and changed everything. He could not promise certainty, but he knew this: the boy deserved more than a life of isolation, looking after a grave in the mountain.

Eventually, Chamboko's words prevailed. The royal wives agreed to remain, but they could not ask the infant to grow up in such desolation. Chamboko would take him to Chiweshe, his ancestral land far away in the land of the people of the Great Zimbabwe. There, he vowed, he would raise the child as his father, his late master, would have wished.

The wives wept as they released the boy and his mother from their sacred pledge.

Chamboko Chiweshe's great grandfather came to Rimuka, the king's court and trading center in Matonganyika, as a trader and had never left. He found his way into the king's court where he became a runner. Over the years, his wisdom came to the attention of the king. Thereon he was engaged by the Lion king's father as a counselor. He married and had a son who was Chamboko's father. The son grew up in the king's court and learnt the ways of Matonganyika and he, too, was engaged by the king as his servant-guard and keeper of his charms. In the reign of the last king of Matonganyika, Chamboko inherited his father's position in the court. He was a most trusted servant; it was on the strength of his position with the late king that vaMatinenga, the queen mother, the late king's host wife, agreed to let him take Tarwa and his mother to the land of Chiweshe.

Soon thereafter Chamboko and his charges, the boy, Tarwa and his mother, vaMarunjeya, embarked on the long journey to the land of Chiweshe. It was a hard journey which saw them walk along riverbeds that flowed with African blood and valleys that bedded the bleached bones of the dead. Destruction, devastation and tears watched them silently in the ghostly villages and forests that had lost even the song of birds. The villages along the way, the once proud lines of clans and families living in the tradition of their ancestors were now no more than rubble and little hamlets squatting on white men's farmland. The cattle and the harvested fields had all become war booty for the white hurricane, the vanquisher.

Months later, they arrived in the land of Chiweshe. It had not been spared. Chamboko had no home to come to. The white hurricane had ravaged and scotched the land and its people as it had the land of Matonganyika and its neighbours. Rain had followed and swept their carcasses off the face of the earth. Their tombstones were the broken-down hovels squatting around the fields of white men's farms that stretched forever without boundaries.

The country had changed. African tongues, once proud, now subdued, greeted them with unfamiliar accents. Chamboko stood in stunned silence, staring at the land that had once been his father's. It lay quiet, resigned to its plunder.

A sunburnt white man now ruled as chief, presiding over African farm labourers. They were black, yes, but not the Chiweshe people Chamboko had known as a child. These men did not speak the language of his ancestors, nor did they answer to his totem. Their totems were strange to Chamboko's ears, Nkosi, Tembo, Mhofu, Nyati, Mulauzi…. They were different yet they shared one haunting truth: they were all remnants of an Africa that had vanished. Their cracked lips and hollow eyes told the story of a life drained of honour, of a future stripped of meaning. They were ghosts of a land once alive with song, now silenced by conquest.

Chamboko and Tarwa's mother joined these hordes of hungry orphaned natives and worked on the white man's farm for food and shelter.

Chapter Three

In the land of Matonganyika of old, little boys grew up together. Their days were spent playing in the valleys below the mountains and along the rivers, playfields where the adventures of childhood and the memories of youth were made. They molded clay bulls and smashed them in bull fights against each other. They built swings in tall trees and dared each other to soar as high as the heavens. They slid down the weather-beaten smooth rock and splashed into the Matonga River, swimming deep into its sandy bottom. They played warrior wars with dry stalks of maize, and shields made of grass. They hunted the forests and snared the hare and young deer. They picked *tsubvu, hute, tsambatsi, tsombori,* and *maroro* - the plentiful wild berries of the African tropical forests. They befriended the old cows as well as the tough young oxen and rode their backs like tamed horses. They coxed the fat-udder milking cows to submission and sucked hot jets of fresh milk from their udders with skillful hands into their own mouths just like calves. They contested each other's marksmanship with catapults shooting down soaring eagles in mid-flight. They learnt the ways of Matonganyika manhood from each other.

It was a childhood Tarwa, the son of the last king of Matonganyika, the late King Chokwedu, would never have.

He grew up on Chikwepa's farm where children and adults were farm hands. His mother, vaMarunjeya, once a dignified figure within the royal court, who was used to a life confined to shaded quarters as she served the king, now toiled in the tobacco fields. Her frail body, unaccustomed to physical exertion, struggled with the demands of hard labour. vaMarunjeya and Chamboko, his guardian, were up at sunrise and in the fields of tobacco before the infant Tarwa opened his eyes each new day. He grew up under the shady trees at the edge of the fields where his mother left him to sleep while she worked.

By the age of five, he too was a farm hand earning his keep. Like the other children on the farm, he was a water carrier following behind the hoe swinging labourers with buckets of water to quench their thirst in the hot sun. When he grew older, a hoe was placed in his hand. Thenceforth he was expected to plough his quota like all adults.

Every season brought its share of farm work to be done. In all seasons, daylight was for work and nighttime for rest waiting for daylight. There was no tradition of community nor life outside the daily toil in the fields that left them all so tired that they collapsed to sleep soon after the evening meal every day.

Chamboko raised the boy as well as he could - teaching him the ways of Matonganyika. However, the boy, though humble by nature, had a spirit which naturally wore its royal heritage like a second skin. Chamboko had been a servant, he could only teach the boy to grow up to be as good a servant as himself. As the king's servant-guard and keeper of his charms, Chamboko was well informed about sorcery. Along with that knowledge was also his naturally superstitious nature. He passed on his superstitions and knowledge to the boy. vaMarunjeya, the boy's mother, taught her son the totem of Matonga clan, their Matonganyika kingdom and their genealogy beginning with his father, Chokwedu to Zharara, their founder father, who sat on the Supreme Council of the Ancestors.

Tarwa learnt well.

As with all storms and all things in life, the hurricane dissipated by and by. In its wake metamorphosed a European government and way of life that forever changed the face of the land. New towns came. The old Great Zimbabwe and its edifices was ignored and relegated to the dust of yesterday. The towns came on bicycles, smoke belching motorcars and wiggling trains.

New houses, the likes of which had never been seen, were built in the town. The houses were multistoried and soared high into the sky like mountains. The stores and houses of the towns had lights that shined like lightning making night as bright as day.

More Europeans came demanding more African servants and labourers. The call went out to the villages and the farms, Africans were needed in the towns to work - labour to carry the building timber, labour to mold the bricks, servants to make tea the Europeans would die without three-cupful- doses-of each day and servants to nanny their children.

The farms lost out to the towns. A strong backed obedient African could work in the town half as hard and make twice as much money and more. Those of them who returned to visit their village homes in the country told glorious stories of the wanders and the generosity of the white men in the towns.

They returned to their villages loaded with gifts of blankets, sweets, tea and baked bread for their relatives. Some bought bicycles and others returned with enough money to begin restocking the cattle their families had lost in the tumultuous plunder of the white hurricane.

Tarwa grew up in those times of change. His life, however, had no vision beyond the horizons of the farm and its endless fields of tobacco and maize. Chamboko and his mother were the pillars of his young life. The white farm owner, nicknamed "Chikwepa" for his ever-present tobacco pipe, was pleased with their work and left them alone.

However, the order and peace in their life ended abruptly. One day, the ancestors turned their back on Tarwa's mother, vaMarunjeya. They were weeding a row in a tobacco field when she suddenly keeled over like a felled tree and collapsed in the hot sun. Chamboko, who was working alongside her shouted for help. They all rushed over to her, but she was beyond help. The water they poured on her face to revive her, fed the soil, and the air they tried to fan around her remained as hot as the sun it came from.

She died before their eyes.

Tarwa, the quiet boy, roared with the pain of his loss. He held his mother to his chest and shook her violently to bring life back into her dead body. He called his dead father to help. He did not hear him. Like a man possessed, he let his mother's body drop to the ground and lashed about the tobacco plants in the field. Everyone scampered out of his way until Chamboko gripped his hands and held him to the ground. Chamboko chanted Matonga accolades to pacify the bereaved boy. Eventually he calmed him down. The chant had invoked Tarwa's place in history. He fell into the euphoria of his ancestral Matonganyika past glory. The chant recalled his father and praised the boy as the seed bearer of the Matonga of Matonganyika of tomorrow; his mother like his father would live through him.

Chikwepa, the white farm owner, rushed over and saw vaMarunjeya's dead body lying on the ground. He ordered them to lift her and take her to the compound so that they could continue with the day's work. No one responded to his command. They all stood rooted as far away from the corpse as possible. He shouted his order again, but it moved no one. The fear that held them rooted where they stood was far greater than the weight of his command. In the end, he too stood rooted in the periphery of the dead woman's shadow, unable to comprehend the fear that was in his labourers' eyes.

Chamboko was the first to speak. He pulled Tarwa to his feet and shouted to the onlookers that whoever had killed vaMarunjeya would pay dearly. Hysterically, he declared that he was Chamboko, guard of the king's charms, he knew how to deal with witches and wizards.

Chamboko's outburst awakened Chikwepa to the cause of the fear that had gripped his labourers.

"Stop talking nonsense! No one killed that woman!" the white farmer admonished Chamboko.

But no one believed the white man.

Chamboko and Tarwa lifted vaMarunjeya's body and carried it to their hut in the compound. They lay the corpse on the floor and covered it.

They immediately left the farm and took the road to a *nganga* who lived in a village quite a long distance from the farm. They found the *nganga,* who greeted them well with sympathy for their loss.

He gave them his condolences.

After they had settled down, the *nganga* took his *hakata,* (the bones of divination) from their pouch which was in the folds of his garment. He threw the *hakata* repeatedly on the ground, shaking his head all the while. Chamboko and Tarwa sat transfixed to the *hakata* searching for the revelation that only the *nganga* knew.

Finally, with deliberate solemnity, the *nganga* gathered the *hakata* from the floor and slid them into the worn leather pouch and put it back in the folds of his garment. That act, quiet and resolute, signaled that the *hakata* had spoken, and their message would neither be questioned nor reinterpreted.

He faced them and spoke with conviction: the *hakata* had revealed that Tarwa's mother, vaMarunjeya, had fallen victim to a malevolent curse cast by a jealous, barren woman, an old witch who lived on the farm. This was the same woman, he claimed, who had robbed other mothers of their newborns, taking life from the wombs aborting their children, all because of envy.

Tarwa, he explained, had once escaped her witchcraft before because he had not been born on the farm. But now that the boy had grown and blossomed, the witch's jealousy had reignited. Unable to bear the sight of vaMarunjeya's joy, she had struck her down, ensuring the mother would not witness her son grow into a man.

The *nganga* had no need to say anymore. There was only one

such old childless woman on the farm, she had to be the witch.

In the old days when Chamboko was the king's servant-guard and keeper of his charms, he would have hurled the accursed woman before the king's court and exacted justice. On the farm, however, it could not be done. The last person who had accused the old woman of witchcraft had been driven off the farm with a severe whipping by Chikwepa, the white farmer.

Chamboko could not risk the wrath of this stupid white man who dismissed witchcraft and sorcery as primitive nonsense. All he could do then was to protect the boy.

They returned to the farm and buried Tarwa's mother without pointing a finger at their suspect.

By quiet consensus - spoken only in glances and whispers, everyone on the farm except the white man knew what had truly claimed vaMarunjeya's life: sorcery. No one dared say it aloud, but the belief hung heavily in the air like smoke.

Anyone who might have suggested that vaMarunjeya, frail and worn from working in the relentless tobacco fields, had simply collapsed from sheer exhaustion or related causes would have been dismissed as a liar, someone covering for the old witch. In the eyes of the labourers, any death except by the hand of another was the work of sorcery.

After the burial, they returned to the *nganga*. Chamboko wanted to remove Tarwa from the farm immediately, but he had no place to send him. He turned to the *nganga* to resolve the boy's imperiled future. He asked the *nganga* to inoculate Tarwa against the evil of the witch and make him resistant to all future machinations of evil. The *nganga* obliged. He made tiny cuts on Tarwa's chest with a thin shaving razor blade and rubbed a thick mixture of baobab roots and animal fat into the cuts. The boy screamed in pain as the mysterious medicine hit the blood in his veins. The *nganga* smiled to himself, Tarwa's screams were a good indication that the medicine was working.

Then in the dead of the night with only the stars to guide them, the *nganga* led them into the forest and sacrificed a white chicken without a blemish in its white feathers and doomed it to carry the evil spell of the witch forever. Thereafter, he led the boy to the river where he gave him a purification of water which he did by spraying the water upon Tarwa's body with the tail of a lion. The inoculation and purification of the boy was completed by a call to the late King Chokwedu and his ancestors to protect their seed and sweeten the world for his maturity. Tarwa became a man. They spent the rest of the night at the *nganga's* abode.

In the morning, the *nganga* took Chamboko aside and told him he would do something about the witch on the farm in his own time. He then ordered that Tarwa leave the farm and go to Salisbury, the town, and work there.

It was as if the *nganga* had reached into Chamboko's mind and plucked out the very thought he'd been too afraid to voice. The idea of sending Tarwa to Salisbury had flickered in Chamboko's mind before; he'd heard stories of men, young and old, making money there. But the town loomed large and menacing in his imagination, a place ruled by white men whose cruelty he had tasted firsthand. His first encounter had been seared into memory: the hanging of his master, a spectacle of violence that left him wary of ever stepping into their world.

Still, Tarwa was different. Young enough to learn, old enough to work without constant supervision. Chamboko hesitated, torn between fear and hope. But the *nganga* was resolute. He told him that the ancestors had visited him in the night, their voices clear and commanding. Tarwa must go, he said. The ancestors had spoken. Salisbury would not swallow the boy; it would bless him.

It was all a great relief for the old guardian of the king. He paid the *nganga* two British pounds for his great work and returned to the farm with Tarwa to prepare for his journey to the town.

The night of their parting came a week later. Being as divinely sanctioned and blessed as the journey was, Chamboko had no difficulty in finding a man to take Tarwa to Salisbury and look after him until he found work. The man he found to take Tarwa was vaMahwata, a family man from a nearby village. He had lived and worked for white people in Salisbury ever since the white people arrived. Thus, Tarwa was going to be in experienced hands.

"I have found a good man, vaMahwata, to take you to Salisbury to help you find work." Chamboko told Tarwa.

"The town? What about you?"

"Me? I am an old man. For now, my life is here on Chikwepa's farm."

"No, we must live together. You have always said that my father and you were inseparable. We should be together."

"We shall be together when you have your own village and king's court, with your own cattle, your own wives and your own children who will be my grandchildren."

They stared at each other in the semi-darkness of the hut in silence.

The next day, in the evening, after the day's work in the fields, Chamboko called Tarwa into their hut. Tarwa, who had just received his monthly wage of two shillings and six pence from Chikwepa, thought that his old guardian was calling him to give him the ritual monthly advice about saving his two-shillings-and-six-pence wage. Instead, Chamboko asked him to sit down and presented him with a brand-new pair of khaki shorts, a shirt and a blanket, all which Chamboko had bought from the farm store on credit. Tarwa had never had anything new, let alone a pair of pants, long or short. To thank Chamboko, he put his hands together and began to clap them in the tradition of his people, but Chamboko silenced him.

"Listen to me," he said.

"Hongu sekuru (*Uncle*)." Tarwa responded.

"Things are not well for you here. As you know your mother is freshly buried. Your own ears heard what the wise *nganga* said about the evil that caused her death."

"Hongu sekuru."

"I buried your father, the Lion. I have buried your mother. I don't want to bury you too. It is the young who should bury the old. Do I make myself clear?"

"Hongu sekuru."

"There is nothing I would have liked better than to have you live with me on this white man's farm, at least for a little while longer, until you are fully grown. But I cannot disobey the will of your ancestors. The wise *nganga* told me that it is the wish of your ancestors that I send you to Salisbury. This place is too dangerous for you. I don't want to have your blood on my hands. I am only your guardian; I am not a Matonga. Your people dictate what you do. You know that don't you, Matonga?"

"Hongu sekuru."

"Anyway, look around you. Look at this white man's farm, what is here for a young man like you? Uhh? These white men's farms are for old people and young men without a head on their shoulders. Not you, you are a man of royal blood. The future of Matonganyika is in your loins. You could never save enough of your monthly wage of two-shillings-and-six-pence to buy cattle or marry a woman with that pittance that the white man pays us. Your father is looking forward to his grandchildren and the return of his land from you. Don't disappoint him."

Tarwa looked down at the floor and found he had nothing to say. Thoughts of the faraway land that had been his ancestors' flooded his mind.

He knew that Chamboko was right; however, the thought of leaving him behind ached his heart.

The future was cloudy, but the present held even less promise. He had no ties to the farm.

His mother and Chamboko had told him enough for him to know that the farm was only a place of temporary refuge which would be replaced by other places until he had his own village to start building Matonganyika clan again. He thought of his mother's grave which would forever tie him to the farm and Chamboko who would always be his only relative even though they were not related by blood. With these thoughts in his mind, he found it hard to accept that the farm was only a place of refuge. It was his home, the only home he had ever known - cutting himself off from its familiarity was painful.

Later that evening, Chamboko, with dry haunted eyes sent Tarwa into the compound to buy a clay pot of rapoko beer. They sat with the pot of beer between them and Chamboko sang Matonga songs with the painful vigour of anguish and alcohol. Tarwa drank a small gourd-full and spat out the beer. He could drink as well as Chamboko had taught him, but his mind was a jumble of fears that strangled his throat. He slept while Chamboko sang himself hoarse until he, too, fell asleep where he sat. When Tarwa woke up, he found Chamboko asleep with nothing covering his body. He pulled the new blanket Chamboko had given him, over Chamboko's body, and went out into the night.

He found himself on the foot path that led into the forest behind the compound.

Blindly, his feet carried him through the darkness of the overcast night and brought him to the nondescript mound of soil that was his mother's grave marked by a stone. He collapsed over it. Tears gushed from his heart like torrential rain breaking through an angry cloud. He shook violently.

Tears flowed onto the stone on the grave as he abandoned himself to his mother. In his pain, the only word that floated through the tears was *"amai, amai, amai..!"*

After what seemed like an eternity, his heart emptied itself of all tears it held. Only then did he feel the discomfort of the stone under him. He stood up and walked to a nearby *msasa* tree.

He sat down and crossed his legs. He put his hands together in honour and respect to his ancestors of Matonga and began to pray saying, "Kings of kings, chiefs of chiefs, magicians and messengers of the Creator, my fathers, I am alone. I am an orphan. I have no father or mother. I have no breasts to suckle from nor a home to call my own. Help me find my way. Help me on this journey to the white man's world. I beg you. Please bless me. My father, CHOKWEDU, I call on you to take my prayer to your father, MUROVE: Murove, my grandfather accept my plea and take it to your own father, CHIKANDA, the great hunter: Chikanda, hear me and take my words and prayer to your brother, the great chief, TAPERA: Tapera, take my word and prayer, I beg you to carry it to your father, my great, great, great, great grandfather, DUMBURA: Dumbura, the guard of the people and kingdom of Matonga, take my tears and prayer to MAISANGO and his father GWENHURE. GWENHURE please finally take my request, my prayer and lay it all at the feet of the great one, ZHARARA, our founder-father who sits on the Supreme Council of the Ancestors and ask him to present to our Creator, Our God, my prayer for I am only a child, an orphan, the only one left. My Lords, hear me."

He clapped his hands for the last time and heaved a sigh of relief. He had passed his prayer through all stations of his ancestry; the rest was up to them.

Chapter Four

Tarwa joined the flood of wide-eyed displaced Africans heading into the town of Salisbury. It was a long journey to Salisbury on foot, but the journey was a stroll for him. His youthful enthusiasm and prospects ahead took over and numbed him to fatigue and the painful memory of the recent death of his mother.

The town was built in a valley around the mountain of Harare. The Europeans called it Salisbury, a name from England, their mother country. The Africans stubbornly called the residential area of the town designated for Africans, Harare, a corruption of the name of the Harava people whose land the town was erected on. It was a new world full of wonderment for Tarwa. He had heard stories about the town but nothing in his life had prepared him for the immensity of wonders that enveloped him in Salisbury. The white farmer back in Chiweshe, Chikwepa, the only white person he had ever seen, was of a reddish sun burnt colour almost as red as some of the native African people. The white people he encountered in the town, however, were of a pink colour and they all looked alike. The roads were as wide as some of the dry rivers he had seen in Chiweshe. The glass-windowed stores full of imported merchandise seemed wall less. He could see people inside reflected in many mirrors, each person having his own double.

His first encounter with a motorcar could have been a bloody affair had his new guardian, vaMahwata, not pulled him off the road. Tarwa was so fascinated by the speeding bicycles, the horse drawn carriages and the motorcars on both sides of the dusty road that he took leave of the good sense he was born with.

They arrived at vaMahwata's lodgings in the Old Bricks section of Harare in National, where all Africans in the town were housed. It was a huge dark room with two holes in the wall that served as windows. The cave-like room was built of cinder blocks with un-plastered walls. It was divided into six rectangular spaces, separated by pieces of cloth strung on cords nailed to the walls. All but one man slept on the bare concrete floor. The same man with the bed also had a primus stove that filled the room with the smell of paraffin when he lit the stove to cook. The rest of the people in the room cooked their meals outside behind a communal bath-toilet hall. There were ten rows of these huge rooms, each row carrying a line of fifteen. The toilet-bath halls were strung in between every five rooms in line and they stunk. Outside the entrances, flies buzzed all day in the stench that hung in the air: inside, overflowing buckets of urine and excrement from the tenants always surpassed the buckets capacity. The tenants were used to the flies and the stench, Tarwa learnt to live with it as well.

vaMahwata lost no time with Tarwa's education of the town and the ways of its people. He spent their long journey to the town teaching Tarwa the ways of white people and what they expected of their servants.

He took the young man into town the next morning, reminding him of all he had taught him along the way. At the District Council Offices, vaMahwata paused and helped Tarwa acquire his *chitupa* - the registration document that permitted an African to live and work in town. With the stamped paper in hand, vaMahwata turned solemn. "First, get your white employer to sign you into work," he said. "And never leave home without it." The warning was stark. An African found in town without a *chitupa* was thrown into jail.

According to vaMahwata, who worked as a houseboy for a white family, it was easy for an African to find work in the town. The kitchens and gardens of white households were waiting for servants. Any place where there was a white person, there was sure to be employment for an African. The only qualification needed, vaMahwata said, was the African's willingness to shout "baas" or "madam" when called as well as the African's generous surrender of his hands, back and feet. Thus, there was bound to be employment for one as well-endowed as the strong-backed Tarwa.

The guiding spirits of the ancestors led Tarwa to the Dominion Building where he was promptly hired as a porter-tea boy. Mr. Jim, the white *"baas"* who hired him decided, however, that the solemn name "Tarwa" which the boy had been given by his late father, King Chokwedu, was no name for an African working for white people. Without fanfare, he told the nervous but most grateful Tarwa that hence forth he would be known as "Edmond", a proper English name befitting an African working for him.

With his new name and the spackle of wealth to come in his eyes, Tarwa, now called Edmond, entered the employment of Mr. Jim. His job routine was straightforward and well defined. He was to sit in the little room that served as the kitchen at the end of the passage and ensure that there was a plentiful supply of hot tea for all the Europeans who worked in the building. He was also told to keep his ears peeled to the passage ready to respond to any European voice calling "Edmond", "Boy" or any other name or sound that indicated that a European needed a hand, a back or foot. It seemed that most of these Europeans had abandoned their own natural physical attributes and demanded their African servants provide theirs for their comfort; Edmond gave his most generously.

It was not long before Edmond became a master at making the English tea Mr. Jim had hired him for. He learned to put the right amount of sugar and milk in the individual cups that he soon won the hearts of all the white people in the building. He was a zestful worker. He ran where others shuffled their feet. He was everywhere in the building giving a hand and even helping the sweeping and maintenance crew although that was not his job.

He learned to speak a version of broken English which he adapted from his guardian vaMahwata. His English would have been comical had it not been spoken by one so charming and disarming as Tarwa was. vaMahwata taught him to preface every address to every white person with "baas" and "madam" and to punctuate his dialogue with a liberal sprinkling of "please's" "yes please baas" and "yes please madam" with his head slightly bowed. This disarming servility was rewarded with "keep the change" whenever he returned with any pennies in change from an errand. Some white people in the Dominion Building even gave him their cast-off English winter weather clothes.

Time passed quickly. Days became months. He missed Chamboko, but he didn't miss the farm. The streets of the town made him curious about the fancy things in shop windows. But he never bought anything. He only used his money for rent, food, and the small packages of groceries he sometimes sent to Chamboko whenever vaMahwata went back home.

He had no time to visit Chamboko although he longed to. He hired himself out to white people on weekends and worked their gardens and cleaned the floors. In return they gave him another steady income and free food.

He worked in Mr. Jim's house as well; however, he was so grateful to Mr. Jim for hiring him at the Dominion Building that he always refused any wage for the work that he did at the house. He gladly polished the floors of the house and did anything else Mr. Jim told him to. Mr. Jim, a bachelor, took him home in his motorcar on weekends when no one else needed work done and had him clean the house and the week's dishes. They did the gardening together because Mr. Jim enjoyed taking off his shirt to work in the garden.

Sometime after his first year working in Salisbury, Edmond became due for leave. The week before his leave was due, Mr. Jim took him to his house on a Friday after he had locked up the Dominion Building. As always, Edmond slept in the empty servant's quarters at the edge of the backyard of the house and woke up early on Saturday morning to work. Mr. Jim slept late on Saturdays, so Edmond started with the floors and the dishes waiting for Mr. Jim to get up. When he did get up, they went into the garden, where they watered the vegetables and the flowers and weeded the lawn. The work took them all day. When they finished, Edmond took the tools to the shed and washed himself in the shack at the back of the servant's quarters. He returned to the yard to tell Mr. Jim that he was leaving. Mr. Jim was standing inside by the kitchen door. A brand-new Raleigh bicycle was parked by the door. Edmond thought nothing of it.

"Edmond!" Mr. Jim called him.

"Yes, please baas." he replied walking towards him. Mr. Jim came outside and stood resting his hands on the bicycle handles.

"Can you ride a bicycle?" Mr. Jim asked.

"No, please baas."

"Well, it's time you learned. I'm going to teach you, my boy."

Edmond grinned sheepishly. He had always wanted to ride a bicycle. But bicycles were expensive, and among the poorly paid African labourers and houseboys in colonial Salisbury, they were a rare luxury.

"Common boy. Get up here." Mr. Jim said with a challenging smile.

"I fall please baas." Edmond said hitching up his trousers.

"No, you won't, I'll hold it for you."

Edmond gingerly climbed onto the saddle. Holding onto the handlebar for dear life, he waited for Mr. Jim to push him into motion. Mr. Jim urged him to paddle and pushed him. It was fun. He was at once fascinated and afraid. He paddled but the greater the motion came from Mr. Jim's push.   "Take it to the road and don't look at me. Look where you are going!"

"Y-e-s please b-a-a-s!" he shouted into the wind, paddling and hanging on.

Mr. Jim continued to push as they raced down the gravel road. Edmond bit his lip and paddled with the motion coming from Mr. Jim's push.

Suddenly, the bicycle became lighter, and Edmond stole a glance behind to check on Mr. Jim. He was alone. Mr. Jim was way behind. He panicked and pulled the brake - the front brake. The bicycle pitched forward and hurled him into the air.

"*Maiwee* please baas!" Edmond screamed as he bit the dust.

Mr. Jim crumbled into the dust road in fits of laughter that would not stop.

Edmond was embarrassed but the pain in his bruised leg was stronger than his embarrassment. He lay in the dust groaning.

Eventually, Mr. Jim stopped laughing and got up and came to him.

"So, how do you like your bike?"

"Bike for me?" Edmond groaned.

"Yes, bike for you." Mr. Jim said helping him up. "I bought it for you, you mutt!"

Suddenly, Edmond's leg didn't hurt anymore. Instead, he felt so happy that he couldn't find the right words to thank him. He shouted to his ancestors, asking them to see the wonderful gift they had given him.

"Baas, please, for me?" he asked again.

"Didn't I just say it's yours?"

Edmond heard what Mr. Jim said but he still could not believe his ears, he stood and stared at the bicycle.

"Go on, pick it up. You can learn to ride it on your own."

Edmond, dazed but happy beyond words, picked up the bicycle and followed Mr. Jim back to the house.

Chapter Five

Early in the morning, vaMahwata gently woke Edmond. It was the first day of Edmond's three-week break from work. But Edmond was already awake. He was too excited to sleep! He couldn't wait to go back to the farm in Chiweshe and see Chamboko again. He had continued to lay down, but he was not asleep. He had laid awake for a long time waiting for the first sign of waking activity from the other lodgers sleeping in the room so that he could get up and take the road.

He threw off his blanket and jumped from the reed mat they slept on. He quickly dry-washed himself with a wet towel and wiped the sleep off his eyes and dressed. vaMahwata helped him load two suitcases, crammed full of clothes and gifts for Chamboko, vaMahwata's family and their *nganga*, on his bicycle carrier. They tied them securely with string and shook hands. It was a little before daybreak when Edmond mounted his bicycle and bid vaMahwata goodbye.

The sun was barely above the horizon when Edmond cycled his way out of town. vaMahwata's direction was easy to follow since there was only one main road out of the town to the farms in the northwest.

He cycled furiously and made good time. Pleasantly, he remembered the first time, more than a year ago, when he had travelled the road coming to look for work. He was a boy then travelling on foot, now he was a young man, a deer in flight, riding a bicycle. By noon he passed the first section of white farms and entered African villages that divided Chikwepa's farm from the nearest white neighbours. He ate up the distance with his speeding, heavily loaded and delicately balanced, bicycle. The valleys were no problem going up or down, he was a strong young man. He fought the steep inclines without much ado. However, the sandy footpaths were another matter. The bicycle wobbled and fell twice when the suitcases refused to cooperate by staying in place on the carrier.

The most difficult part of the ride came when he branched off from the main footpath and cut across the forest to use the cattle paths. The sand was loose, and the trees stood branch to branch. He was forced to walk the bicycle until he rejoined the footpath at the boundary of Chikwepa's farm.

It was quite late in the afternoon when he finally entered the section of the farm where the farm workers lived. It was a very hot day, but the occasion had dictated that he dress his best despite the hot weather. He rode his brand-new Raleigh bicycle into the compound draped in a heavy blue woolen blazer and tie, a pair of long flannel trousers, dusty but well-polished black shoes and a pair of sunglasses hanging on his nose. All but the shoes and glasses he wore were English winter weather cast offs from the white people he served tea and pottered for at the Dominion Building. He looked and felt like an important man.

He wiped the rivulets of sweat from his face with one hand and held the bicycle with the other. The front wheel twisted in the furrow of sand in the much-travelled foot path at the entrance into the compound. He jumped off in time to avoid an embarrassing fall and caught the bicycle. He looked around. No one had seen him yet. He was relieved.

He pushed his bicycle through the deep sand and made it into the compound to Chamboko's hut. He suddenly realized that he was the only soul in the compound. His heart fell.

He had made his grand entrance into the farm compound at the wrong time of day. There was no one to see him arrive in his fine clothes, no one to admire his bicycle chariot and no Chamboko to surprise.

Disappointed and tired from the long ride, he resigned himself to the forlorn reception of the empty compound. He rested his bicycle against the hut and sat down in the shade.

He fell asleep.

As the sun began to go down, a trickle of farm hands returning from the fields streamed by. One of the farm hands recognized him and sent word to Chamboko who was behind. The old man raced as fast as his legs could carry him.

"Tarwa! Mambo Wangu (*My Lord*)! Matonga!" Chamboko shouted.

Edmond heard his name called in his sleep. He woke up abruptly, embarrassed. A gallery of excited faces and jostling bodies stood around him. He sprung to his feet and fell into the arms of Chamboko who had broken through the bodies.

"Sekuru! Sekuru Chamboko!" he shouted in Chamboko's embrace.

Hands and bodies pressed forward to touch him and hopefully greet him. The farm hands were excited and all claimed to know him. Soon there was no room to breathe. "Give them room." a considerate voice shouted above the clamour. Repeated calls to give them room finally prevailed but the old man clung on with tears in his eyes. His lips silently murmured whispered accolades and prayers of thanksgiving to the ancestors for Edmond's safe return. Amid all the jostling, they looked at each other. Edmond had grown and assumed the tall strong body of his father. He was dark black with a face breaming with confidence. Chamboko looked ageless, he had neither grown older nor younger. His lithe body stood erect where other farm labourers stooped from their days bent over the fields of tobacco.

Edmond may have chosen an inopportune time of day to arrive at the farm compound, but he had surely arrived on the right day. It was a Friday evening, next day Saturday was a half day at work. Friday was the prelude to the weekend merry drunken nights that always continued into Sunday, the one day the farm hands did not work the fields.

Word of his arrival became the toast and excuse for the drinking binge that ensued in the compound. Not that there was any desperate need for such an excuse, Saturdays and Sundays were their days to drink to excess. However, Edmond's spectacular brand-new Raleigh bicycle, his spectacular European clothes and the voluminous suitcases sagging on the spectacular bicycle's carrier demanded honours.

No one from the farm or the surrounding villages had ever returned from Harare with so much. And certainly, none before him had ever returned with a brand-spanking new Raleigh.

In all his years on the farm, Chamboko had never been one to socialize with the farm hands. He worked side by side with them in the fields but kept them at arm's length. To Chamboko, the former courtier of the Lion king, the farm hands were inferior, and even more so to his charge, the royal blooded Tarwa. What sociability he had allowed them, he had totally withdrawn at the death of Tarwa's mother. This attitude continued even after the old woman they had suspected of the witchcraft that had killed Tarwa's mother, had fled from the farm.

His general opinion of the farm hands was that they were envious and sorcerous. Edmond's momentous return had caught him off guard. However, it was not for long. The farm hands with their cups of beer offers to Edmond, as well as their open admiration of his clothes, bicycle and the wonders they expected his two suitcases to contain, jolted him back to his true self. He stood up resolutely and grabbed Edmond's hand.

"Tarwa is tired and hungry. Thank you very much for your company but we must now go inside so I can feed him." he declared proudly.

The farm workers, ever so careful around the eccentric old man, voiced no objection to Chamboko's stopping their party around his hut. Chamboko's party may have been over but theirs had just begun. They carried their pots of beer and regrouped elsewhere. Chamboko could ask them to move from his hut, but he most certainly could not stop them from talking about the bicycle and Edmond's clothes.

Edmond helped Chamboko take the suitcases and the bicycle inside and closed the door. Without saying a word, Chamboko shook the door to ensure it was securely locked and satisfied himself. He then took a pinch of *mbanda*, an incense so strong, he believed, no evil spirit could stand its smell. He burnt the incense to purify the hut. When the incense had burnt out, he formally greeted Edmond with a prayer to the ancestors.

Chapter Six

Edmond had three weeks of leave from work: time enough to explain to Chamboko that he was no longer called Tarwa; time enough to take the old man on a fanciful mental journey through the streets of Salisbury, dazzling him with tales of the town's wonders; time enough to speak broken English and teach Chamboko to pronounce words he did not understand; time enough to impress him with the affection "his white man," Mr. Jim at the Dominion Building, had showered upon him; time enough to beat his chest and declare that he, Edmond Tarwa Chokwedu, was the only African in Harare with a brand-new Raleigh bicycle; and most importantly, time enough to satisfy Chamboko that indeed, the ancestors had blessed him.

More than a year had passed since Edmond left the farm, a long, lonely separation for both him and Chamboko. They only had each other in their lives. Their history, and the tragedy that had set them in the world they found themselves in, made it impossible for either of them to live his life without the other. The boy had grown to maturity and become a young man. The ancestors had been kind to him and blessed him beyond either's expectation. He had brought home to Chamboko fifty British pounds in cash for safe keeping, money which Chamboko had hastily counted and recounted and buried in a tin in the floor of the hut. As Chamboko buried the money, he whispered a wish to the ancestors, that they bless the young man with just two more good years. Enough time to earn enough money to buy some cattle, pay *roora* (bride price), and build a village to start to reclaim their royal legacy. The old man looked at Edmond with pride. The young man had the hunky stature of his father and confidence of royalty in his face. The one thing he was most grateful for was Tarwa's new name, Edmond. He practiced saying it silently. He thought it was a blessing that the young man's employer had given him a white name. He called him Edmond, not everyone was called Edmond. It was a special name which meant his white man had adopted him, a mark of favour, a sign that the ancestors were guiding and protecting the young man.

Edmond's first mission on the second day of his arrival at the farm was to visit his mother's grave and offer his prayers to the ancestors on her side of the family. He cleared the weeds and added stones onto the grave's bed. When that mission was finished, he found himself without much to do. He dressed in different clothes every day and kept his tie firmly knotted on his neck, just as his boss, Mr. Jim, did. He put on his sunglasses and rode his bicycle to the river to wash himself and his bicycle daily. When that was done, he would ride to vaMahwata's village and spend the rest of the day visiting the family.

He spent his evenings under the magical tongue of Chamboko drinking rapoko beer with him and recounting the glories of Matonganyika. They sang songs about the hunt and the war they lost. He listened to the legends and the words of the songs with new interest. He cried for his father and vowed to make him proud of him.

Two days before his return to work, Chamboko took Edmond to the *nganga* who had cleansed him when he left the first time. They arrived at the *nganga's* village on Edmond's bicycle with Chamboko sitting on the carrier. Edmond, dressed in his English winter weather clothes, was a testimony of the *nganga's* success and blessings he had garnered for him. Edmond, with profuse gratitude, had brought the *nganga* some gifts. The *nganga* received the gifts with praises to Edmond's Matonga ancestors and promised never to forget him in his prayers to the spirits for continued good luck. The *nganga* cleansed Edmond again at the river and finished the cleansing by rubbing the oil of good luck on his forehead. Edmond was ready to return to Harare.

Chapter Seven

The years following Edmond's employment at the Dominion Building were steady and even more prosperous than the first. The ancestors blessed him and gave him good health. He worked as industriously as ever.

Mr. Jim increased his wages and gave him free reign with his work. Edmond could have easily made friends with the other Africans working in the building but, like Chamboko, his mentor at the farm, he kept to himself. Chamboko never ceased to warn him of the evil in people especially other Africans. He accepted no food, drink or even a cup of water from his fellow workers who, Chamboko had convinced him, had to be jealous of his position.

At home, in the Old Bricks where he continued to live with vaMahwata, he cooked the food and washed the pots in deference to vaMahwata. He could have afforded to buy a primus stove and a bed as others had done, but he did not. What Mr. Jim or the other white people he served at the Dominion Building did not give him, he did without. vaMahwata was of a similar frugal bent. He lived a singular life in the town working and saving everything for his large family in the village in Chiweshe. vaMahwata and Edmond admired each other. vaMahwata had everything that Edmond wanted in his own life - he lived on the traditional land of his people where he had his village, three wives, children, land to plough and a few head of cattle. vaMahwata held Edmond in the highest esteem and felt most complimented by the younger man's admiration. However, for all his good fortune of traditional land and family, vaMahwata had his own sorrow. He had many children but none of his sons showed the promise and ambition Edmond had. His daughters were industrious but what good was a girl to Mahwata's family name? Girls would get married and move on with their husbands taking their husband's names. He encouraged Edmond in all his work and gave him the advice of a father to a beloved son. He distrusted people but not as much as Chamboko had instilled in Edmond. He discouraged the young man from excesses in his belief in witchcraft and sorcery, however, on that score he did not fare well, his advice came too late in Edmond's life - one cannot uproot and replant a tree that has already set its roots in hard soil.

&

As the years went by, Edmond progressed, and his savings grew making him a prosperous young man. However, his progress and prosperity did not bring him peace of mind. Rather, it brought him restlessness.

He was ready to start a family since he had now amassed over three hundred British pounds. It was enough money to marry many wives with, buy cattle and build a village. Despite his wealth, he felt empty unable to take the next step of his life to get married and start his own family. The weight of his royal ancestry, the mystery of the life he left behind as an infant and the question of his own future as the son of the late King Chokwedu filled the gulf in his mind with confusion. That gulf refused to close, refused to let him make the simple decision to settle anywhere but in the land of his forefathers.

He confided in Chamboko, voicing both his yearning and the storm of uncertainties that had taken root in his mind. Chamboko, steeped in memory, lived as though the present were merely a shadow of the past. He spoke of life through the memory of his days at court as the king's servant-guard and keeper of his charms, the high position he had lived in of ceremonial rituals bound by traditions now forgotten. In doing so, Chamboko stoked Edmond's longing to return to Matonganyika, the ancestral land that was calling him in silent whispers only he could hear. The more Edmond expressed his dissatisfaction with his circumstances and landless existence, the more Chamboko drew the young man's thoughts backward into the land of the past. Listening to Edmond, one might have thought he had lived that life himself. His words mimicked Chamboko's own words confidently describing a world he had never lived in.

Edmond saw the land in his dreams; he heard voices from the past and conjured visitations from his father in his sleep. Whenever he related his dreams to Chamboko, the old man sang accolades and interpreted dreams and visitations as the call of the ancestors to return to the land of Edmond's birth. It was easy for Chamboko to convince Edmond of these beliefs and soon he had the young man seeing his life anew in the yesterday gone. He belonged in Matonganyika, his people were calling him home.

Edmond's work for Mr. Jim did not suffer from his restlessness but the white man noticed the haunted faraway look that came to his eyes. He asked Edmond what troubled his mind, but Edmond pretended that all was well with him, Mr. Jim let the matter rest. vaMahwata, who shared a sleeping reed mat with Edmond in the Old Bricks, saw signs of a man troubled and headed towards insanity. Night after night, he heard the young man talk incessantly in his sleep calling the dead in the middle of the night. vaMahwata, like Mr. Jim, asked Edmond what the matter was and received the same blank answer. For long periods, Edmond hardly slept. He spent restless nights talking, supposedly, to unseen spirits until vaMahwata felt compelled to warn him of the evil that fell upon those who called the dead in the night. It frightened Edmond. He was aware of not only the danger that lay ahead if he did not stop but also of the confusion he suffered. However, he could not help himself. The more he learned from vaMahwata of his nightly rumblings, the more difficult it became for him to maintain his composure by day. He lost his appetite and his health suffered.

Finally, vaMahwata, using his influence on Edmond as a father figure, suggested to him to consider asking for leave from Mr. Jim, his employer, so he could go and get some rest. But Edmond didn't dwell on the suggestion. Instead, he made a firm decision: to leave his job for good. He had all the money he needed to build his village, stock it and get married.

He approached his employer, Mr. Jim and handed him his *chitupa* asking him to release him from his job. Mr. Jim listened to Edmond's incoherent reasons with sympathy but without conviction. He felt that all Edmond needed was a long rest. Instead of signing him off, Mr. Jim returned the *chitupa* and granted him an indefinite leave of absence.

Chapter Eight

Edmond left Harare with all his possessions and went back to the farm. He consulted the *nganga* and received much encouragement on the course he had chosen to follow.

Edmond, who was a healthy young man, began to feel a heaviness in his left hand. Then he started feeling an itch in the palm of that hand. In the palm of his left hand was what he had always assumed was a natural birthmark, something he was born with. The itch was so persistent he began to think of returning to the *nganga* to get some explanation or treatment to stop the itch. Finally, he told Chamboko about the problem with his left hand and the itch he was feeling.

Chamboko sat him down and looked at the hand and examined the "birthmark". After examining the mark, Chamboko shouted and sang praises to King Chokwedu.

"Oh, forgive me! I had completely forgotten all these years." Chamboko said to the bewildered young man.

"What?" Edmond was perplexed.

"This is your father's mark, a symbol of your royal lineage!"

"What does that mean?"

"When you were an infant, newly born, in the mountains of refuge, the King inscribed this symbol there with the point of his specter, the royal staff, a sign of your lineage."

"Uh? So why does it itch now? All these years growing up it was just there. It did not do anything. Why is it itching now?" None of it was making any sense to the younger man.

"It's the King calling you home. It will all go away once we get back to your kingdom." Chamboko advised him confidently.

Edmond did not understand it.

"What about now? I cannot walk around with this constant itch in my hand. Should we not go see the *nganga*?"

"Matonga, my young prince, there is no need to go see the *nganga*." Chamboko said gleefully.

He assured him that this was just a sign that the ancestors were calling Edmond to come back to Matonganyika to start rebuilding the old kingdom. He went into the bushes and picked some herbs and mixed them with a pinch of snuff tobacco and rubbed the concoction on the royal lineage mark in Edmond's palm. Edmond felt a sensation of heat in his hand which somehow stopped the itch.

However, try as he may, Edmond did not share Chamboko's enthusiasm nor the excitement that his royal lineage mark itching was a cause for celebration. The voices he had heard in his sleep in Harare had deserted him on the farm and doubt sat in their place. A premonition that he could not explain overcame him. When he had asked Mr. Jim to sign him off from his employment, he thought he was sure of what he wanted to do. Now in the empty chamber that had become the gulf that had overflowed with dreams of Matonga kingdom, a voice of gratitude echoed. The gratitude was with his boss, Mr. Jim, who had refused to let him close the door. He could always go back to his job. For that, he thanked Mr. Jim with all his heart. Chamboko had no such doubts. He danced with joy when Edmond returned from Harare and told him that he had left his employment. The news was the happiest he had heard since the fateful day when he made the trek that had brought them to Chiweshe. Back then, he had surrendered his future to ancestral blessings. But even as he did so, he quietly harboured the hope of one day returning to Matonganyika to revive the old kingdom. He doubted that there would be anyone there still alive but that did not discourage him, Edmond would marry and start anew.

Patiently Chamboko had watered the seed of the plant in the younger man's mind to return to his father's homeland. He was convinced that the ancestors were with him in his pursuit to persuade Edmond to return to his fatherland. They had been with him all along when he was raising Edmond. Through this young prince, Chamboko saw his own life restored to its former position of king's servant-guard and keeper of his charms. He believed that the ancestors always took care of those who followed the tradition of their fathers. He had lived by that dictum and protected his own prince soon-to-be king, Edmond, as his father and father before him protected their own. Now the ancestors had proved themselves true. Tarwa was now called Edmond - a living proof of the hand of the ancestors. He had been blessed with the royal physique of his father with enough personal wealth to return to the tradition of his people. He, Chamboko, would see the royal young man become the new "Lion", King Chokwedu's successor and therein, lay his own destiny.

&

Chamboko was all for loading everything they possessed on Edmond's bicycle and towing it on their journey back to Matonganyika. Edmond entertained the idea but convinced the old man that it was impractical. With the nightly dreams of return to his fatherland that hand haunted him in Harare gone, his enthusiasm was dampened by the uncertainty that had replaced them. He suggested that they only take the things which they would need for the journey and return for the rest. Chamboko reluctantly agreed.

The day before their departure, Chamboko visited the *"baas boy"* (boss's boy), the African foreman of the farm workers, carrying a clay pot of beer. Of all the men in the compound, the *baas boy* was the only one Chamboko deemed worthy of his respect. The *baas boy* felt honoured by the visit; after all, Chamboko was the guardian of

Edmond, the wealthiest African on the farm, who owned a bicycle and dressed in expensive European clothes.

During the visit, Chamboko informed the *baas boy* that he and Edmond were leaving on a journey to attend to family matters. He did not elaborate, but he wanted the foreman to be aware of his absence. As the meeting ended, Chamboko issued a solemn warning: should anyone attempt to enter his home while he was away, a curse worse than death would befall them.

The *baas boy* understood. He nodded gravely and bid Chamboko farewell.

The next morning, they left the farm. They woke up at early dawn and prayed to the ancestors. They asked for protection and guidance and ended the long exultations with each taking a pinch of stuff that had been dedicated to the ancestors.

The suitcases with their clothes were securely locked and stacked up against the wall. They hoisted Edmond's bicycle up the sooty thatched roof and tied it to a cross beam to protect the tires from the moisture on the floor. They counted three hundred and eighty British pounds and put three hundred pounds in the tin and reburied it in the floor under the fireplace and covered it with ashes.

Apart from the *baas boy* he had met with the night before, Chamboko had no close friend to bid farewell. Nor did he trust any of the compound's neighbours to safeguard his home during their absence. His only protection lay in the *baas boy's* word, passed along to the other farm workers, that Chamboko's hut was not to be disturbed. Any violation, they were warned, would invite consequences steeped in witchcraft, worse than death.

He locked the door and left the fate of their possessions in the hands of the ancestors.

&

They left with eighty British pounds in Edmond's pocket, two bundles that contained a blanket for each, food provisions of *chimkuyu* and *mangai* (dried beef and boiled salted maize), a bottle of water and two English weather overcoats.

Sunrise found them beyond Chikwepa's farm, and they would have continued making good time if their route had not become so circuitous after the familiar foot paths on the farm ended. White farms bordered each other with wire fences that ran unbroken lines. The two men were forced to detour from their planed route. Chamboko was familiar with the terrain, but he could hardly recognize the route he had taken so long ago when he had brought Edmond and his mother to Chiweshe. The villages that marked the land had vanished and succumbed to the wilderness.

Long fields of tobacco and maize crops drying in the harvest season-sun stretched forever inside the wire-fenced farms. They walked all morning following animal and hardly travelled human foot paths.

Occasionally they walked into frightened wild game, but they met no human soul, nor did they see any villages. The sun followed their progress and became unbearably hot with the afternoon. They quenched their thirst with water from the bottle but that did not relieve their fatigue. They walked until the wild forest suddenly stopped at the edge of a long wide road.

Chamboko was amazed by the length and breadth of the road. It slumbered its way in either direction east and west into the horizon. He wondered out loud, asking where the long road was going.

"I don't know where it's going," Edmond replied, "but I am sure it's the same road I ride my bicycle on when I go to Harare. The town is full of big roads, bigger than this one."

Chamboko let the sleepy road take his mind to the Old Bricks, Edmond constantly talked about. "You think this road could take us all the way to where you lived in Harare?"

Chamboko asked with the enthusiasm of a child.

"Yes, yes it will." Edmond said looking up and down the road with a light in his eyes.

The road gave him an idea he had not thought of when they made their preparations for their journey. The idea started with Chamboko's question about the road taking them to Harare. He thought of the possibilities of the road taking them to Harare. He thought of the possibilities of the road taking them where they were going. There were no tire marks on the road, but its width and breadth suggested that it was made for motorcars. Edmond smiled.

"Sekuru, let's rest for a while under the shade of that tree." He said pointing at a *mukwa* tree that was on a sand bank along the road.

"There are thicker and better trees ahead, let's walk on a little further." the old man suggested looking at the skimpy shade the tree cast.

"*Kwete sekuru*, they are all the same. It's better we rest here." Edmond cajoled the old man.

Chamboko wanted to argue but the sun had sapped his energy. He climbed the sandbank and took the weight off his feet in the shade. Edmond looked towards Harare and hoped a motorcar would come by and give them a lift. He had money to pay for a lift. He climbed the sandbank and sat down beside Chamboko and soon fell asleep under the hypnosis of the forlorn wide road.

They slept a while and the sun moved on. As it tilted to the west, it deprived them of the tree shade. Chamboko was the first to wake up. The sting of the sun's rays had pierced through his closed eyes. He shook Edmond.

"Has a motorcar come?" Edmond asked, jumping to his feet

"What motorcar? Are you dreaming?" the old man asked jumping to his feet.

"Oh, I thought I heard a noise." Edmond said, scanning the empty road.

They gathered their bundles and prepared to continue their journey. A noise down the wide road came to Edmond's ears. He dropped his bundle on the ground. The noise was the distinct drone of an engine shimmering in the hot afternoon air.

"That's a motorcar engine! What did I tell you?" Edmond shouted excitedly, pointing in the direction of the sound of the engine.

"Stop playing with me. Let us get going there are no motorcars in the forest."

Chamboko said picking up his bundle.

"Wait, wait, may be the motorcar will carry us."

"Are you mad? Why should it carry us? Does it know where we are going?"

Edmond jumped off the sandbank and stood by the roadside waiting for the motorcar to appear. When it did, he waved his hands frantically.

The motorcar, a black Ford Model T, with a rhinoceros horn mounted to the hood, came up the wide road in a hail of dust denser than a herd of cattle fleeing a leopard. The driver, a pipe smoking white man, breezed past the open-mouthed Edmond without looking at him.

"My ancestors' spirits, a motorcar! A motorcar, here?" Chamboko threw down his bundle in disbelief.

"But he didn't stop. He didn't even stop." Edmond was distressed.

"Why should a motorcar that doesn't know you stop? and a white man too..."

"But..." Edmond was deflated.

He had told Chamboko many stories about white people and how they all liked him. To his chagrin, the first white man they had met together outside Chikwepa's farm had proven him false. He picked up his bundle and followed Chamboko.

The rest of that day's journey was dominated by the conversation about the motorcar that had refused to stop. Edmond swore that he would stop the next motorcar that came and prove to the old man that he had not told tales. Their journey cut a virgin path through the forest on the other side of the wide road. Chamboko did not check his bearings anymore because the big mountain, DETEMBWE, which was miles away, loomed in the far distance. All they had to do was keep it in sight.

They walked in silence after they had exhausted the subject of the motorcar and kept their eyes ahead and their ears alert to any rustle of leaves that could mean the presence of the snakes.

The fading evening sun caught them in the thickness of the forest with no sign of any villages anywhere in sight. They hurried to find open ground to make camp before total darkness closed in.

Chamboko found it for them. He climbed a tall tree and spotted a hillock further on that had little vegetation around it. They made it to the spot before the last rays of the sunlight disappeared. It had a jutting rock facing the hillock which gave them a natural windbreak. Chamboko leveled the grass around the rock with his feet while Edmond gathered wood and made a fire.

When they had settled down, Chamboko roasted *chimukuyu* and divided it equally with Edmond. It was a filling meal, eaten with *mangai* and washed down with water.

Chapter Nine

After the meal, Chamboko started to tell Edmond a story from the past as he usually did but fear of the night held his tongue. Chamboko, a man of many superstitions, believed that in a strange place like the hillock in whose shadow they had camped, unseen spirits could come and steal his voice. He pulled the overcoat tightly over his body and lay down to sleep on his blanket. Edmond did the same.

The jutting rock was a solid windbreaker. The warm glow of the fire flowed between them and made them as comfortable as they would have been in their own home.

The night sounds of the forest died down and left a complete silence until Chamboko started to snore. However, Edmond's sleep was not disturbed by it, he had lived all his life with Chamboko's snoring.

Deep in the night, the peace under the moonless sky was shattered by the volcanic roar of a lion.

Edmond screamed as the roar died down.

"Shsssss! *Hush!* Shsssss!" Chamboko ordered Edmond to keep quiet.

The lion roared again. Its earth-shattering thunder came closer. Edmond barely managed to clamp his hand over his mouth to stifle himself from screaming again. The dark forest had come alive with unseen monsters.

Chamboko peered in the darkness to determine the lion's position. It roared again and Chamboko turned to face the darkness. It roared repeatedly, each roar seemingly sounding closer and closer. The two men stared in the darkness in the direction of the roar. When their eyes became accustomed to the darkness, they saw the outline of a lion sitting on top of the hillock. Chamboko sat up with his feet tucked under his thighs and began clapping his hands loudly. He chanted to the spirits of the ancestors.

"King of kings, we hear you," he shouted chanting into the darkness. "We know you are a father watching over his children. We thank you."

He turned to Edmond, "Are you a fool? Clap your hands!" he chided.

The lion roared. Edmond recovered his wits and joined Chamboko clapping his hands.

"We are your children on a sacred journey. Thank you for walking with us. We hear you. We see you. We thank you." Chamboko voice was even and reassuring. Edmond fell in line with every word Chamboko uttered and responded to each of the lion's roars. All sleep left their eyes, for Edmond it was as if the lion was threatening to crush the hillock with its roars and only their entreaties were forestalling it.

The lion's roars and their responses went on until dawn when the lion left. With the lion's departure, they drifted off to sleep and woke up shortly thereafter with the sun. The experience of the night had taken Edmond's tongue. As he stomped the few remaining embers of fire, he wanted to talk about the night, but fear gripped his jaw shut.

Chamboko spoke in a low voice, urging Edmond to hurry and extinguish the fire. His face was somber, betraying none of the fear that had drained the colour from Edmond's face. They gathered their bundles and resumed their journey, walking in silence through the dew-heavy grass that brushed against their legs. The landmark mountain, Detembwe, that guided them did not seem any closer than the previous day, but their route was easier to negotiate. There were no farm fences to be seen. Chamboko assumed that they were either too deep in the middle of a farm, or they were walking through an unclaimed forest.

They came upon their breakfast when they found a patch of *maroro* along the footpath. They were yellow and ripe. Chamboko and Edmond sat down and devoured them voraciously savouring the berries' cool juices. It was an invigorating meal.

They resumed their journey with added speed. Edmond had by now worked up enough courage to ask Chamboko the question that had troubled him since dawn when the lion left.

"Sekuru, what happened last night?" he asked Chamboko as he followed his footsteps.

"Uh?" the old man grunted.

"What was that last night?"

"What was what?"

"The lion." Edmond said fearfully, as if the very mention of the beast would bring its deafening roar back.

"Why do you ask a question that you already have an answer to yourself. Edmond, you are a grown man not a child." Chamboko continued walking as he talked but Edmond was not satisfied. The old man had evaded the question.

"Sekuru, if you don't explain to me what happened, and how it happened, how am I to know the things of grown men?" he shouted angrily.

"It was a spirit of the ancestors. Now keep quiet, you shouldn't talk about such things. They are sacred." the old man said firmly and walked on.

Edmond resigned himself to Chamboko's evasions. He

shrugged his shoulders and accepted the mystery.

They came upon a small stream. The water was sky blue and little fish glistened in its shallow sandy bed. The two men were not thirsty, but the cool clear water induced thirst in their mouths. Edmond emptied the bottle and refilled it with fresh water while Chamboko drank it in gulps directly from the stream. Edmond drank some too with his cupped hands and sighed with satisfaction.

They crossed the stream and followed a natural footpath that passed between two old giant fruitless *mihacha* trees. The two trees may have been shorter than giants but the other trees surrounding them seemed to have been trimmed to accentuate and leave the two to soar above them. Their tops were flat and green in sharp contrast to the two old leafless *mihacha* trees. It was such an unusual sight that Chamboko, who knew better than to comment on the unusual in a strange forest, caught himself just in time to bite his tongue.

He stopped suddenly in his tracks. Edmond bumped into him and almost knocked him over. He looked ahead and saw what Chamboko had seen. He opened his mouth to scream but fear defeated his voice. He stared at the two trees in terror.

A huge lion stared at them. It was old. Its mane was grey with age but it's long face was fierce. It reposed on the ground between the two giant trees and stared at them. Chamboko kept his eyes locked into the beast's intense stare and gently pulled Edmond telling him to sit down. They both did and Chamboko repeated the chant they had shouted all night.

"*Changamire,* (Your Highness) King of kings. We see you. We are your children..."

Edmond clapped his hands in unison with the old man and kept his eyes on the huge animal. A fear he had never known, a fear worse than he had experienced the previous night overcame him.

In the dark, he had only imagined the immensity and ferociousness of the beast, in broad daylight and at such close range, what he saw had no words in his imagination, the reality before him was overwhelming. He abandoned Chamboko's prayers and said his own to his dead mother, calling her to come and save him from the beast. The lion continued to stare at them and yawned without a roar. Chamboko continued to chant but the lion seemed disinterested. Chamboko repeatedly stated his name and Edmond's, indicating that they were its children on a sacred journey. The huge beast sat and stared without moving. It looked like a statue carved in stone.

Chamboko's hands grew weary and numb from clapping, but he did not stop. Clapping as if their life depended on it, Chamboko praised the ancestors and thanked them for the lion's presence. Towards sunset, the lion lifted its heavy bulk and sauntered off into the forest disappearing with the sun. Chamboko clapped his hands once more and sighed with relief.

The initial fear Edmond had experienced had paralyzed him. He had kept his eyes on the huge beast, and some force emanating from it had wrapped him and dragged him through the cold fire in its eyes. He had lost consciousness of the ground he sat on and the sun that was shining. He was in the belly of the ferocious beast and therein he lay, dead.

They sat where the lion had left them, each lost in his own thoughts until the receding sunlight turned into an amber evening glow.

"Get up and gather some firewood." Chamboko said quietly.

Edmond did not respond. Chamboko nudged him and repeated himself. Edmond found his voice and retorted, "I am not going into those bushes."

"You may have a beard, but you are still a child." Chamboko

said dismissing Edmond's fear. He got up and gathered the dead wood that was around them.

"Pick up my things and follow me." Chamboko told Edmond and walked towards the stream, away from the two giant *mihacha* trees. Edmond followed with their bundles.

Chamboko lit a small fire and asked Edmond if he was hungry. Edmond shook his head and spread his blanket on the ground near the fire and laid down. Chamboko sat by himself and stared at the flickering flames with nothing to do.

He had no desire for food himself either. Edmond closed his eyes. He was neither awake nor asleep, but his mind had fled from the forest around him. He was back in Harare in the comfort of his work and safety of his home in the Old Bricks. It was a relief that brought him some sleep.

Chamboko woke up with the first strands of sunlight that filtered over the treetops. He stretched and yawned in the crisp air. He started to walk to the stream when he saw a herd of antelope emerging through the path between the giant *mihacha* trees. He hid behind a bush and watched them trot gracefully towards the stream. He peered over the bush and saw the antelopes join the other animals at the stream. There were hares, wild pigs and others he could not distinguish from where he hid. It was a pleasant sight to behold. He stayed hidden from the game until they all watered themselves and disappeared.

Edmond woke up with the aroma of roasted *chimukuyu* in his nose. He rubbed his eyes and met Chamboko's brimming smile.

"Matonga, you woke up at last. You people who live in town sleep so much." Chamboko said amicably and began to hum a merry song. Edmond could not reconcile the dark resolution he made during the night with the happiness Chamboko radiated. He got up and walked to the stream to wash himself.

"We are going back, aren't we sekuru?" Edmond asked when he returned, finding a spot to sit beside the fire.

"Uh?" the old man grunted as he always did when he was going to say no. However, that did not stop Edmond from saying what was on his mind.

"We are going back, aren't we?" Edmond asked again, looking into the old man's eyes.

"Going back? Why?"

"Why? Don't you see it yourself? The road is full of wild beasts. It's dangerous for us to proceed."

"Matonga, who knows more about these things, you or me? Have I ever led you astray?" Chamboko's voice was firm.

"No, but we keep running into unmentionable things, I am afraid."

"Did I not teach you that your father was a lion? Didn't your mother tell you the same?"

"She did..."

"Are you telling me you are afraid of your own father who is protecting you? Yes, I agree the path was closed yesterday. But it was closed because there was danger ahead. Maybe there was a leopard or some vicious snake waiting to spring on us? If you had been up this morning with me, you would have seen all the animals of the world at the stream. This is sacred ground we are sitting on. The forest beyond those trees must be enchanted. Be happy, you have your ancestors looking after you."

Edmond was not impressed.

"If all you say is true, mind you I'm not saying it's not true, but if all you are saying is true, why am I afraid?"

"Thats because you are not as old and as wise as I am."

"Sekuru, I respect you and what you say, but I want to go back to Chikwepa's farm and return to work for Mr. Jim..."

"My ancestors," Chamboko declared, "you don't know anything do you? Here I am setting up your life as your father and your people would want me to and there you are mouthing the talk of babies saying you want to go back. Matonga, think like a man." Chamboko said with finality and began chewing a piece of meat.

Edmond rarely disagreed with Chamboko. He respected his wisdom and followed all his advice. This time, however, he disagreed. The ancestors had always been a source of comfort for him, not the fear that was now in his heart. He realized that Chamboko was clearly intimidating him with age and experience. His explanation of the lion was plausible if he knew what the lion had meant by its appearance and its ferocious roars. Was it not also possible that his own explanation and the voice he kept hearing in his mind were correct? Was it not plausible the road was closed because his ancestors wanted them to turn back? He weighed the two possibilities and accepted his own. He decided that he was not going a step further. That decision, however, sat comfortably in his mind for no longer than a fleeting moment. Chamboko was a determined man, he was not going back with him. He would be alone. He reconsidered and came face to face with his own cowardice - could he brave the wilderness alone and risk meeting the lion again without Chamboko's bold cadence.

"Sekuru, please let's go back." Edmond pleaded.

"Uh?"

"Please..." Edmond was close to tears. Chamboko ignored the

plea and glared at him.

"Matonga, I always thought you were a man, like your father. Now I see I was wrong. But I will not let childish fear stop our work. I am here for you. I will protect you as I have always done. I have taken care of you since you crawled on all fours since you were a baby and I will continue to do so. All I ask of you is that you let me do my work. Just follow my advice and leave the rest to me. If you do as I tell you, we will be all right. However, if you don't, you will bring the wrath of the ancestors on our heads. Now finish eating, we have a long walk ahead of us."

Edmond found it difficult to swallow the sawdust the meat in his mouth had become. He forced it down and threw away the piece in his hand.

Chamboko tried to make light of their disagreement, but it was in vain. Edmond kept his eyes at his feet until they stood up to leave. Chamboko started to walk towards the enchanted forest following the path that led to the two giant trees, but Edmond refused to follow him. He declared that he was not going anywhere near the trees.

They compromised on an alternate route and followed the stream until they cleared the thickness of the enchanted forest they were circumventing. Edmond plodded behind the old man bumping into the undergrowth. His body was moving but without the aid and guidance of his eyes. His eyes were otherwise engaged, searching for the unseen waiting to jump on them from behind the trees.

Detembwe became distinct but not any nearer as they trudged on as the day wore on. Chamboko still had no idea how far they would have to walk before they reached their destination. Whenever Edmond asked him to estimate the distance, the old man truthfully replied,

"I don't know but it is up ahead."

Chamboko could not estimate the distance with any certainty because when he had travelled to Chiweshe with Edmond and his mother, Edmond had been a baby and a delaying factor. They had stopped to rest for days, sometimes weeks, and in one case, a whole month whenever they had come upon a village with people and food. Now the villages had vanished with their former inhabitants and hostile white men farmers stood in their place.

Chapter 10

They cleared the enchanted forest and turned into an animal path that cut directly towards the mountains. They soon found themselves in a dry riverbed. It was clear of trees, but its sandy soil had yielded to thorny bushes.

Edmond felt secure in the open riverbed. He asked Chamboko if they could spend the night there and the old man agreed, if only because he was still trying to allay Edmond's fear.

They spent an uneventful night and started walking before dawn. Chamboko explained to Edmond that if they could only reach the mountain valley he would know how much further they had to go. It was an incentive that worked. Edmond had reconciled himself to continuing the journey, at least for that time. He took the lead determined to make it to the nearest human settlement before leaving Chamboko and returning to Harare.

The sun followed them with intense heat, but Edmond ignored it. His fear and prospect of finding an inhabited settlement spurred him on.

The land began to decline as the trees thinned out. Gradually they found themselves in the fringes of a valley. They came upon a herd of cattle grazing in the green grass. It was the most welcome sight for Edmond. Cattle meant people, and people meant protection from the wilderness and its beasts. He climbed the nearest tree and looked up and down the valley. The herd of cattle was thick and covered the whole valley as far as his eyes could see, however, there were no cattle herders, the people he was looking for. He sat in the tree to the bemusement of Chamboko who was resting under the tree. After a time of desperate searching, his eyes saw a wide stretch of what looked like sand. He determined that it had to be the wide road they had last seen the day they had left the farm, two weeks ago.

He climbed down with a new purpose.

"Let's move on sekuru." Edmond said picking up his bundle.

"Why don't you like this shade?"

"Let's move on and cover more ground."

Chamboko had no argument with Edmond's newfound enthusiasm. They walked through the herd of cattle wiping cattle flies from their sweat-caked face. At the edge of the valley, the forest thickened again but it did not deter Edmond. He was determined to make it to the road before sunset. And they did. When they reached the wide road, Chamboko looked at Edmond.

"So, it was the road that was calling you, uh?" Chamboko said understanding why Edmond had led him at such a hectic pace.

"Maybe a motorcar will come."

"Forget the motorcars. Where would they be going out here?"

"I don't know but we will find out."

They built a fire, ate and slept by the roadside.

Since the road was going in the direction of Detembwe Mountain, Chamboko, who would have preferred cutting through the forest using footpaths, had no argument. Edmond walked without the fast-paced determination that had brought them to the road. He was hoping a motorcar would come along. None did - not for five days, anyway. They walked and slept by the roadside keeping the mountain in their sight.

It had been a week since they had been on the road, and no motorcar had passed in either direction. Thus, when the early morning twitter of the birds was overcome by the sound of a motorcar engine, Edmond had not been overly excited. But the sound grew stronger and even Chamboko had to sit up and see what it was.

Edmond sprang to his feet and looked for the motorcar. He saw it. It was a lorry struggling under the weight of its cargo. The lorry was quite a distance from where he stood but to Edmond it could have already passed them. He kept waving and called out for the driver to stop. By the time the driver reached him, Edmond voice was hoarse from screaming while Chamboko sat agape wondering what had got into him.

The lorry crawled and stopped beside Edmond.

"Hini wenna funna?" (What do you want?) the white man behind the wheel asked Edmond in *Chilapalapa* a language Edmond understood well from working in town for white people.

"Lift baas please sir." Edmond asked with his head slightly bowed and his hands respectfully put together, in front.

"Funa umsebenzo?" the white man asked him if he was looking for work.

Edmond was too excited to catch what the white man had asked. But not understanding a white man had never stopped Edmond from making his own assumptions before. He continued.

"Yes, please baas."

"Hop in." the white man said indicating the back of the lorry with his head.

Edmond rushed around the lorry and found Chamboko standing. Hurriedly, he told him that he had gotten them a lift. Before Chamboko could reply, Edmond picked up his bundle and blanket and shouted at the old man to hurry.

The white man engaged his lorry into gear and raved the engine threatening to leave them.

Chamboko caught up with Edmond and climbed onto the back of the lorry.

The lorry jerked forward throwing Chamboko into the sacks of fertilizer stacked on its bed.

Edmond helped him up and propped him against the sacks of fertilizer.

Chamboko had never ridden in a motorcar. The brave old man who stood his ground against the monster lion now trembled at the lorry's growl, its engine vibrations rattling through his bones. He felt like a trapped animal. Every instinct in his body screamed to leap out but only Edmond's reassuring voice made him bear it, for now.

Initially, Edmond laughed at Chamboko's fear but as the blood rushed from the old man's face, he became concerned. He talked to him to take his mind off the ground that seemed to be moving under them. The lorry went over a hump in the road and the old man's stomach heaved. All the food Chamboko had eaten the previous night gushed out through his mouth and splattered on the sacks of fertilizer.

"I'm dying before I reach Matonganyika. Edmond, please help me..." Chamboko pleaded.

"Hold on, it's nothing sekuru. You won't die."

He used his blanket and wiped the vomit from the sacks of fertilizer and Chamboko's mouth. He explained to Chamboko that he had seen a lot of people in town get sick the first time they rode in a motorcar. It was the petrol fumes, he added. However, all his explanations did not help Chamboko. He held on to him for dear life.

Towards the end of the day, the road eventually took them to the valley below Detembwe. At close range, Edmond realized that Detembwe was not a single mountain as he had thought; it was a range of numerous, huge mountains each with its own valley. The lorry followed the road running parallel to the mountain range. It struggled with the weight of the fertilizer but kept a steady pace. The lorry would not stop soon enough for Chamboko, but Edmond enjoyed the ride. In the security of the lorry, he had no lions or any other beast of the forest to fear. Added to the security was the convenience of effortless travel. He did not care where the lorry was taking them even if it was in the opposite direction from their intended destination. He settled down and watched the trees go by thinking of Mr. Jim, his boss, and his lodgings in Harare. To Edmond, now, the Old Bricks room he lodged in with all its flies and filthy bath-toilets was in another world only a step removed from heaven, and the land of Matonganyika seemed like the other side of hell. If it was possible, he would turn back now and promise never to think of that land again.

After hours on the road, the lorry turned off and entered another road that was rough and much smaller going away from the mountain range. Chamboko stole a glance to see where the mountain was.

"Where is this thing taking us?" Chamboko shouted over the noise of the engine with a squeak in his voice.

"I don't know." Edmond replied, showing no concern.

"You don't know?"

"Sekuru, don't worry. The white man knows what he is doing."

"I told him where we are going." Edmond lied to placate Chamboko.

The old man had no choice but to believed him. He closed his eyes again. Edmond and Chamboko could not see ahead but it was obvious now they were on a farm. Harvested fields of maize surrounded them and cattle freely roamed the harvested land chewing the de-cobbed maize stalks. The lorry slowed down when they entered what must have been the farmer's household yard.

A big, whitewashed brick house stood at the edge with flowers and fruit trees planted around it. A white woman and her children waved at the driver.

They passed the house and came to a stop at a huge shed leaning against a row of granaries. A gang of shirtless African labourers who were hauling drums of groundnuts stopped and ran to the lorry.

The driver got down and came around to the back of the lorry.

"Plenty, plenty *musobenzo* (work)," he said indicating that there was lots of work for Edmond and Chamboko.

"Yes, please baas." Edmond replied helping Chamboko to get down.

The driver, who seemed to the boss or owner of the farm, called the *baas boy*, an old man of Chamboko's age and told him that Edmond and Chamboko were looking for work and he had hired them.

"Come to the compound with me. I will show you where you will sleep." The *baas-boy* said leading the way.

"What's happening?" Chamboko whispered to Edmond.

"I don't know sekuru, we'll ask this man."

"Wait, wait until the white man is out of ear shot. He may not like you asking questions." Chamboko said walking on his wobbly legs.

They followed the *baas boy* to the labourers' compound. It was no different from their own at Chikwepa's farm.

"You must be hungry; I will give you some food." the *baas boy* offered.

"No, we are not hungry." indeed Chamboko's was not hungry, his stomach was upset.

"Are you sure?"

"*Vakuru* (Elder), can you tell us where we are?" Edmond inquired.

"Oh, you don't know? This is Detembwe Farm." the *baas boy* said opening an empty hut.

"How far are we from Matonganyika?" Edmond continued.

"Matonganyika? Where's that?"

"Sekuru Chamboko, tell him." Edmond turned to Chamboko.

"I don't rightly know from here."

"But didn't you say you'd know when you got to Detembwe?"

"It's that motorcar thing it confused me." The *baas boy* watched them in his own confusion.

"Sekuru, we are in the valley of the mountains, Detembwe is right behind you." Chamboko turned and looked at the mountains as if seeing them for the first time.

"Where did we come from?"

"Sekuru, what kind of question is that?"

"Are we behind the mountains?" Chamboko turned to the *baas boy*.

"*Vakuru*, are we behind Detembwe?"

"That depends, I don't know."

"*Vakuru*, are you saying you don't know where Matonganyika land is?" Edmond asked the question hoping the *baas boy* would say no.

"Are you talking about the B L Mines?"

"What is B L Mines?" Chamboko interjected.

"I do not know what you are talking about. The only other place there is around these mountains are the B L Mines and they are on the other side of the mountains."

The *baas boy* had become exasperated. "Look this is where you sleep."

"We are not sleeping here." Chamboko asserted.

"But my white man said I should give you a place to sleep. All his workers have a place to sleep." the *baas boy* said with obvious pride.

"We are going to Matonganyika."

"I don't know about Matonganyika, I have to return to my work, these people do not do any work if I am not there." the *baas boy* said and began to walk away.

"How about us?" Edmond shouted.

"You can rest, the sun is going down there is very little you can do today. Anyway, our *baas* never works on the day he returns home from town."

"What town?"

"Harare." the *baas boy* said and returned to his crew.

Edmond's face lit up. "Harare," he thought quietly, the white man goes to Harare. All his problems suddenly vanished. The white man was going to be his saviour.

Chamboko sat on the ground and shook his head. His eyes blazed at Edmond.

"Motorcar! My ancestors, now see what you have done?"

Edmond did not respond.

"Now we are lost, and the white man wants us to work for carrying us in his motorcar."

"Sekuru, Detembwe is staring at us, and you say we are lost. Didn't you tell me that you'd know the way as soon as we reached the mountains?"

"On foot. On foot, not in a white man's motorcar. Now I don't know where we are."

When the workday ended with the sunset, Chamboko still had no idea where or how to proceed. Edmond was not worried. He was grateful for the comfort of human voices, of a roof over his head, a door to keep the ferocious beast away and a white man who had a motorcar that was going to be his transportation out of the hell Chamboko was determined to drag him through.

The farm workers came by to welcome them. They all told Chamboko and Edmond how good the white farmer was and how much they were going to enjoy working for him.

Chamboko did not sleep that night. He searched in his mind to find the reason why the ancestors would confuse him so. He found no answer.

Daybreak came. The baas boy shouted, *"Work Time! Work Time! Get Up!"* from the middle of the compound. The farm hands came out of their huts and trooped to work.

Chamboko was ready to continue their journey, but he still had no idea which way they would go. Edmond offered no encouragement for them to leave Detembwe Farm. Foremost in Edmond's thoughts were the farmer, the lorry, and Harare. The *baas boy* had told them his boss made frequent trips. Edmond did not care how long he would have to wait for the white man to make his trip to Harare.

Chapter Eleven

Chamboko and Edmond started working at Detembwe Farm but for different reasons.

Three weeks later, the farmer told the *baas boy* to load the lorry with sacks of maize and to arrange for six men to accompany him to the mines the following day. Edmond overheard the farmer give the *baas boy* the order. He inquired about the trip and volunteered himself and Chamboko to accompany the farmer. The *baas boy* readily agreed to put them on the lorry. The two of them, Edmond and Chamboko, were not putting their hearts into his work, he was glad to be rid of them - even if it was only for that day.

Edmond told Chamboko they had been assigned to the lorry. Chamboko did not want anything to do with the lorry and was about to go to tell the *baas boy* that he would rather not go. But Edmond cajoled and prevailed by telling him that the lorry would take them back to the road which would help to refresh his memory and re-establish the direction they were supposed to take for their journey. Reluctantly, Chamboko agreed.

In the dark hour before the morning, the farmer blew his horn and raved the motor ready to go. The six men assigned to go with him woke up and raced to the lorry. They all carried blankets to keep warm in the open-bedded lorry. This was fortuitous for Chamboko and Edmond, it was an opportunity for them to take their bundles with them in case they decided not to return to the farm.

With the six men wrapped up in their blankets in the back, the farmer sitting alone in the cab, guided the lorry over the rugged road. By daybreak, they found themselves turning into the road running parallel to the mountains.

Chamboko suppressed his fear of the vehicle and began the lone vigil to find a mark on the land around the road that would return his sense of direction. Edmond slept peacefully.

The farmer drove all day, stopping only once to let them relieve themselves in the bushes. The road took them around the mountains and meandered off the valley into the dense forest on the other side.

Chamboko's confidence returned with each mile they travelled. The country was becoming familiar. He told Edmond the good news, but the younger man was not happy. Chamboko's elation was going to take him back to walking through the forest.

Around sunset, a sign reading B L Mining Company appeared on the side of the road. Soon after, they cleared the forest.

The land, as far as they could see, had been cleared of all trees and grass. Huge mounds of brown and white sand stood like little mountains around steel beams that jutted into the air. There were wheelbarrows and motorcars parked at the entrance. One of the motorcars was the T Model Ford with a rhinoceros horn mounted on the hood. They drove further into a large compound housing more than two hundred little zinc-topped huts. There were no women anywhere in sight but black men, big and small, in rough khakis and helmets on their heads. The mine store was in the middle of the compound and a grinding mill stood by its side. A white man and his *baas boy* came to meet them at the grinding mill. Chamboko, Edmond and the four farm workers from Detembwe Farm unloaded the sacks of maize and stacked them in the granary. They did not finish until well into the night. After they finished the mine *baas boy* came back and took them to their sleeping quarters.

The sleeping arrangements presented a problem for Chamboko. He was housed with Edmond and one of the four men from Detembwe Farm. He called Edmond and told him to follow him outside.

Edmond followed.

"Sit down, Matonga." Chamboko said finding him a place to sit.

After a long silence, Chamboko spoke. "Matonga, we have arrived. This is the land of your forefathers." his voice was low and grave.

"My father's land?"

"Yes."

"Are you sure?"

"My ancestors, yes, I am sure as sure as I am sitting here."

Edmond looked around, not sure of what he was looking for. He looked at the sky; it was like any other sky on a moonless night. The soil even in the darkness looked the same as any other soil.

"Sekuru, if this is the land of my forefathers, then there is no land."

"Yes, there is. You are standing on it. It stretches from where the motorcar turned off from the mountain to the big river.

"Matonga River?"

"Yes."

"How far is that from there?"

"About five days walk, I am not sure."

Edmond tried to imagine how far five days' walk was and found himself thinking about the wild beasts and not the land they had come to find. Try as hard as he did, there was no sense of curiosity in him, to his mind it was all a mine and a jungle of ferocious lions.

"Five days, that's a lot of land." he said only to disguise his lack of interest.

"My ancestors. That's not all; your land stretches in all directions. It used to take us months to walk from one end to the other."

Despite himself, an interest began to grow in his heart, a month's walk length of land was a lot by any estimation.

"If this is my forefather's land, where is my father's grave? You said you buried him in the mountains. Where is it?"

"It's by the river. As I said I am not quite sure where we are now but in the morning I will know."

They lapsed into silence again.

"Yes, we have arrived Matonga. Praise the ancestors, our journey has come to its end." Chamboko broke the silence, clapping his hands. Edmond joined him.

"We will leave from here in the morning. We will not go back on the lorry now. Woaw, that motorcar will kill you." Chamboko's delight glowed in the dark.

"Forgive me for asking, but sekuru, what makes you so sure this where we are going? This morning you had no idea where we were."

"I told you, I recognized it when we came around the mountain. Now let's go to sleep."

"What will we tell the white man?" Edmond was still struggling with himself.

"You got the white man involved with our journey. You tell him in his language that this is home, we won't be going back with him."

As they walked back, Chamboko tried to see Edmond's face and reconcile it with the obvious doubt and note of disappointment he had detected in his voice but failed.

Edmond did not sleep that night. The knowledge that they had arrived at their destination was both gratifying and unsettling. Indeed, he had wanted to return to Harare many times during their journey, however, now that they had arrived, he wondered why he was not shouting and jumping up and down for joy. If anything, he was feeling empty and more confused than he had been when the whole process started. The land itself, the part he had seen, was nothing but endless sand dunes as far as his eyes could see. There was nothing endearing about it. In his imagination, his forefathers' land was a land of enchantment at least that is what Chamboko had promised. He was frightened of his disappointment, which was as equally discouraging as the fear he now knew he had of the wilderness, especially in the dark.

They woke up in the morning when the first shift of the day was going in.

They followed the four farm hands they had come with on the lorry. Fearfully, Chamboko pushed Edmond in front to tell the white man they were not returning with him to his farm.

"Please baas, we stay." Edmond told the farmer with his eyes cast down to avoid the white man's.

"What the hell are you talking about?"

"Please baas thank you very much. We stay."

"You want to work in the mines now?"

"We stay baas."

The farmer laughed.

"I never thought I would see the day. You want to work here when everyone else that comes to me is running away from this accursed place? You know what B L means?"

"Bad Luck, my boy. Bad Luck. Tell him." the farmer said to one of the four farm hands. The farm hand explained that B L stood for British Lands Mining Company, thus Edmond never got the full import of the farmer's reaction.

Edmond said he understood and repeated that they were staying.

The farmer threw his hands in the air and told them to do whatever they wanted. His four farm workers followed him onto the lorry and left Edmond and Chamboko puzzled.

The moment the lorry disappeared in the hail of dust it churned behind it, Edmond regretted giving in to Chamboko and letting the farmer leave without them.

The harsh reality of the endless mine and its sand dunes hit his eyes in the bright morning sun.

He looked at the strange metal beams fisting the air and the uniformed workers who all ignored them and felt lonely, lost and confused.

Chamboko led the way. Edmond followed. Chamboko asked

whoever would stop and talk to him where they were and everyone looked at him. They replied the same, "This is the B L Mines, personnel office is over there." pointing to a hut at the far end of the compound. Edmond did not try to help Chamboko determine where they were. He was sulky.

Chamboko paid him no attention. He believed that as soon as he established his bearings and led Edmond to his father's court, Edmond would regain his enthusiasm. He continued to ask everyone in sight the same question and they all repeated the same answer. No one had the slightest idea of what he was talking about.

Edmond deduced, however without telling Chamboko, that everyone they had met came from distant lands to work in the mines and thus could not know what Chamboko was seeking.

Chamboko's rescue came late in the afternoon when the mine's *baas boy*, who was also in charge of hiring the mine labourers, finished his shift. He met them at the personnel hut. Chamboko related the journey to him and what had brought them to the mine.

The *baas boy* was a loquacious man, he talked to Chamboko about everything he could think of but the information Chamboko sought. However, during his rumblings, he related a strange story about the mines. He said that the B L Mining Company owned the land from the valley behind Detembwe Mountain to the big river and the banks on the other side. The land, he told them, had rich deposits of gold but they had had problems digging for it because of a series of inexplicable disasters that dogged the mining operations. There were many such inexplicable incidences but the ones that readily came to his mind were the following: mine shafts which had been built and fortified in hard dry soil and rock suddenly turned muddy and collapsed; flames without fires sprouted all over the land without burning a thing, not even a blade of grass; a huge lion roamed the compound and the tunnels of the mine underground, the mine's management (all white men) had tried and failed to kill the lion. They had shot at it but never killed it even at distances closer than five paces - bullets seemed to pass right through it without harm, he told them, there was an old woman who lived in the river valley, in what he could only describe as a hovel.

The *baas boy* himself had accompanied the mine's white men to try and move her, but she had the strength of twelve oxen and the roar of a lion. The lion itself had chased them away from her hut.

The *baas boy* concluded by saying that if this was Matonganyika, the land of Matonga, only the old woman would know.

Edmond was at once fascinated and scared by the *baas boy's* story. He was fascinated by the reaffirmation of everything he had learnt from Chamboko and his mother that he came from a people who are conjurers, who have power over nature. He was frightened, however, by the prospect of encountering the lion again. He now firmly believed that the lion had appeared to stop them from their journey, a journey that seemed, from all indications, destined to end in the dust of an endless mining compound.

Chamboko had sat with his ears riveted to the story. He had no doubt in his mind that they had truly arrived in the land of Matonga, Matonganyika. The strange phenomena that had been recounted confirmed to him that the ancestors wanted to preserve the land for Edmond. The first step towards his mission was to pay the old woman a visit.

He thanked the *baas boy* for the information and inquired about the directions to the old woman's hut and was told that it was a two day journey through the wild forest that began on the other side of the sand dunes.

They were about to leave when Edmond asked the *baas boy* if they could spend the night in the mine compound before Chamboko could say goodbye. The loquacious *baas boy* savoured the prospect of the captive audience Chamboko and Edmond would be for him. That night, Chamboko and the *baas boy* swapped stories and enthralled each other like two excited children lost in a world of fantasy. Chamboko gripped the *baas boy* with the Matonga legends of his time, legends Edmond had heard him tell many times before. The *baas boy* had his own from the far away land he had come from.

While the two old men relived the legends, Edmond reflected on the present and wondered why he had left his job to journey into such an unknown, unseen and dangerous time. The warm glow of his ancestry had turned cold in reality and made him wish he had satisfied himself with the imagined and not tried to live it. If the mine was any part of the enchanted land, not only were they too late to save it, but the magic had also vanished. He fell asleep in the middle of it all.

The *baas boy* woke up early for his shift which was the first of three round the clock shifts. While he was putting on his clothes, Chamboko and Edmond prepared to leave. The *baas boy* opened the door, and a gray blinding mist pushed him back and filled the hut. Chamboko felt his way to the door and pushed it, but it would not close.

"Come and sit down." the *baas boy* shouted to him.

There was no difference between the outside and inside the hut. The mist was impregnable. Edmond sat rooted to the floor, paralyzed with fear.

"What is it? What do we do now?" Edmond shouted hysterically until Chamboko told him to shut up. Chamboko seemed and sounded like the one in self-control but in truth, he was just as petrified. The *baas boy* took it in stride.

"Don't worry" the *baas boy* said, "no harm will come to us."

Chamboko sat down and clapped his hands in the darkness of

the mist calling the spirits of Matonga by name. He chanted the names of the kings and chiefs and abandoned himself to their mercy. Torches appeared outside and voices called on all to stay inside.

"My shift won't be going in this morning." the *baas boy* said, "I better make you some tea to warn your bones."

The tea calmed Edmond's nerves

"Does this happen often?"

"Edmond, Matonga, how often must I tell you not to speak of these things?" Chamboko admonished.

"It happens. Everything happens here." Despite Chamboko, the *baas boy* replied to Edmond.

The mist covered the mine until the darkness of the night took its place.

Chamboko spent the night as he had spent the day, chanting accolades to the power of the ancestors. The *baas boy* joined him occasionally, but Edmond sat mute on his blanket wondering for the hundredth time why he had ever thought of making this journey.

Chapter 12

The next day was bright and clear. Chamboko and Edmond, accompanied by the *baas boy*, left the hut as he led his men to the day's first shift. They followed the directions he had given them to the old woman's hut.

Chamboko walked with the confidence of one at home while Edmond plodded along behind him. Chamboko was full of plans, all of which rested with what they would find at the old woman's abode. They walked through the passages between the sand dunes. When they had cleared them, the sights became familiar to Chamboko. He chattered incessantly pointing to Edmond the various landmarks around and in the distance with anecdotes from his time with the Lion king.

Late in the day, Chamboko told Edmond they were heading to the old hunting lodge and trading post, the place they used to shelter in whenever they hunted with the king in that part of the land. He added, almost as an afterthought, that this was where he had stored some of what remained of the king's personal effects. Edmond followed without comment.

Even for those who had seen the lodge in its prime, it would now take a leap of imagination to believe it had ever been anything of substance. Edmond's first impression was one of disbelief. The rotted beams and ant-eaten grass Chamboko pointed to seemed less like remnants of a once-proud structure and more like logs abandoned there by someone who no longer had any use for them. To Edmond, it felt as if nothing of substance had ever stood there. There were a few charcoals embedded in the soil, two leaning poles that might once have framed a tower or wall, the collapsed remains of a roof at their feet, and wild bushes that now lorded over the rocks and grass that seemed to be out of place.

Edmond looked at Chamboko and decided to reserve his

energy for their continuing journey. He did not expect Chamboko to say they would be spending the night there. But that's just what Chamboko said.

"I know it doesn't look much now but boy we had good times here. Let's rest and build a fire." the old man brimmed with enthusiasm.

"But there's nothing here, not even a wind breaker?" Edmond protested.

"Matonga, we came to build. We don't expect to walk into a house, do we?" Chamboko said forestalling further argument. "Any way we are not sleeping here, but in there."

He pointed to a clamp of trees behind them. The trees were thick and screened off a hill whose top Edmond could see from where he stood.

Edmond's arguments had never held much weight with Chamboko because the older man had always had more wisdom than he did. The progression of their journey from the known to the unknown had made Edmond's arguments even weaker. He conceded and prepared to light the fire Chamboko wanted.

"I have a surprise for you Matonga." Chamboko said with a sly smile on his face.

"What?"

"You know there is a secret cave here?"

"Where?"

"Follow me."

Chamboko walked to the clamp of trees and entered their darkness searching for an entrance.

"Follow me." he urged.

Edmond was not sure that he wanted to follow Chamboko into the darkness he saw in the middle of the trees. Chamboko did not wait for him. He went down on his knees and crawled in. Edmond was left alone standing among the trees. He heard Chamboko call his name telling him to join him, but he declined. As he stood alone among the trees, they too became an intimidation on his nerves. He hurried out into the open and stood looking in all directions afraid to follow Chamboko and afraid to be out there in the trees alone.

After some time, Chamboko crawled out of the tress carrying a large, folded pouch made of elephant hide. His face was a wide grin that stretched beyond his ears.

"Look what I have found for you Matonga! The ancestors are with you." he said with his hands outstretched exhibiting the beauty of the pouch.

"What is it?"

"Some of you father's prized possessions. Sit down and clap your hands and thank him before you touch anything." Chamboko said and put the pouch on the ground.

Edmond approached it gingerly. In the past he would have jumped for joy to receive anything that was of Matonganyika origin, however the pervasive fear he felt about everything stayed his excitement.

"Are you sure it's alright for me to receive this?" he asked, trapped in Chamboko's instruction.

"You are Tarwa, aren't you?"

"Yes."

"Then this is yours. Thank your ancestors."

Edmond sat down and crossed his legs. He clapped his hands loudly and thanked his ancestors for whatever was in the pouch and added a plea for mercy if they were doing anything wrong.

Chamboko opened the pouch for him. Inside it were cured skins of a leopard, an antelope, a zebra and at the bottom piece of the mane of a lion. They looked as if they had just been tanned.

Edmond was mesmerized by the beauty before his eyes. He was speechless. "Oh, there's more, I wanted to see how they looked in the light. Come with me."

Chamboko stood up ready to go back inside.

"But.."

Chamboko waved his hand, "Come, come they are yours. Everything here and all this land even those mines belong to you, Matonga. Come and be with your heritage."

Edmond's curiosity prevailed. He put the precious skins back in the pouch and followed Chamboko.

Chamboko wriggled his way back into the darkness with Edmond behind him, following blindly.

The tunnel immediately widened a few feet inside the entrance. There was a rock above it. It receded upwards leaving them room to stand up straight. A dim light found its way through the crack above the cave where the two rocks parted. The crack was neither large enough to open the cave to the sky nor was it too small to block out sunlight when the sun's rays were angled from the west.

Edmond adjusted his eyes to the dim yellowish light. The ground under his feet was soft and dry with no vegetation.

There were unusual shelves between the rocks that formed the walls of the cave. On the shelves were more animal skins of every description. They were neatly stacked and separated from each other. Spears, muskets and dead gunpowder, knobkerries, shields, starves and a scepter were stacked on their own. On the ground below the shelves were brightly painted clay pots of various sizes. The largest pot lay on its side broken. Its contents, beads, gold nuggets, coins and medallions, were spewed on the ground. Musical instruments drums with crinkled skins curled on the top of their hewed-out trunks, gourds with marimba strapped in, reed whistles and shakers - sat on their own.

As if drawn by an invisible magnetic force, Edmond found himself walking to the wall where the spears and staves were stacked. His left hand involuntarily jerked and reached for the scepter. Suddenly a surge of power raced through his body. He gripped scepter as if it were fused to his palm, the same palm marked by the king with this very scepter when he was an infant in the mountain of refuge during the war.

A chill raced through Edmond's body. Still clutching the scepter in an iron grip, he staggered, lost his footing, and collapsed onto the soft, dusty ground, bellowing and roaring like a man in the throes of dying gasping his last breath. He writhed in the dust, his body seized by convulsions, guttural animal sounds erupting from his throat struggling to breathe.

Chamboko, lost in a reverie of drum-filled days, turned and saw Edmond groaning in the dust. His eyes fell on the scepter clenched in Edmond's hand, and the mark glowing faintly in his left palm. He knew. Instinctively, irrevocably, he knew. The Lion had arrived. Through the portal etched into his son's flesh and the royal scepter forged by ancestral hands, a passage had opened. The spirit had crossed. Edmond was no longer merely Edmond. He was his father now. He was King Chokwedu.

The convulsions momentarily stopped. Edmond's body started breathing normally as he lay prostate looking up as if trying to get his bearings.

Chamboko went and sat down beside Edmond's prostate body and clapped his hands chanting.

"Matonga, come with goodwill. I beg of you, please do not shake your son so. We have arrived. We are most grateful for the safe passage you granted us. Speak to me, I am Chamboko Chiweshe, your servant-guard and keeper of your charms, your trusted servant. I bring your seed, Tarwa, a man as strong as any Matonga that ever walked this land. Speak to me, your word is my command." he clapped his hands.

Edmond bellowed and growled like a lion. His body convulsed again while Chamboko entreated and pleaded with the spirit of the king to settle down: "Matonga, I hear you, ease in on the son you have entered. His body is mortal, be gentle with him."

Another bout of convulsions and bellowing followed. Then Edmond sat up whistling a song Chamboko had heard many times before, the king's favorite song. His eyes had receded into his head and saliva dripped down his lips. Chamboko continued to clap his hand praising the valour of all Matonga.

Still maintaining that tight grip on the scepter, with an authoritative hoarse voice speaking through Edmond's mouth, the king shouted. "Cover me! Cover me!"

"Give me my arms! Cover me!" the voice ordered.

Chamboko scrambled to his feet and scampered to the shelves and came back with the largest piece of animal fur he could find, it was a leopard's skin and a knobkerrie. He put them on the ground before Edmond and draped the leopard's skin over his shoulders and knobkerrie in his hand.

"What is this?" the voice exploded throwing the knobkerrie against the rocks.

"Am I a woman you give a stick to? I am the Lion! I am King Chokwedu! Give me my rifle, hurry!"

Chamboko scuttled back to the shelves and bought a musket with him and gave it to the king. He sat down opposite him.

"May I greet you, Great King, Lord of Matonganyika?" Chamboko asked with a servile voice. The king nodded his head, giving Chamboko permission.

"Greetings oh Great King. Matonga. Greetings to you, who lives in the air, you who hovers the shield that protects us all. Hail Matonga, great, great, great grandson of Zharara who pleased God, the Creator now sits on the Supreme Council of Ancestors! Greeting king and lord of this land we sit on. I humbly greet you."

Chamboko clapped his hands once more and waited for the king's reply.

"I hear you." the king said and fell silent.

Chamboko clapped his hands softly.

"Chamboko, where have you been?" The king asked rhetorically with a pain evident in the voice. "Chamboko where have you been?"

Chamboko was frightened by the question, but an overwhelming sense of gratitude for the king's recognition of him made him smile inside.

"I have been tending to the son you left in my care my lord." Chamboko answered. "I left the family here my lord. I had to take your son to a place of refuge."

"You did well."

The king sat silently for a long time. Then he abruptly leaped up to his feet with the scepter and musket in his hands.

"Follow me. Matinenga is calling. Follow me."

Edmond's body standing up right, had doubled in size. He bumped into the rock above.

"Great King, you are sitting on a body smaller than your own, be careful with it." Chamboko said.

"It's mine. What's a small bump on the head. You have made my son a woman."

"Where were you when my army was destroyed? Where are my children?" the king was not demanding answers but sympathy.

"All your children are with you, my lord. The only one left is the son you sit on. You fought valiantly Matonga, all your people fought valiantly."

"I lost. I lost my children's heritage to the men with yellow beards. I, Chokwedu, Grandson of Zharara, lost the heritage he left the children. I will fight! You haven't seen anything yet."

"I know you will my lord."

"Where are my wives? Where is Matinenaga?"

"I don't know my lord?"

"You don't know? What kind of a servant-guard of the king are you? You don't know anything. Where is Matinenga?"

Chamboko paused for a moment remembering that vaMatinenga was the king's host wife, the queen mother.

The king crawled out of the cave.

The sharp rays of the late afternoon sun blinded the king. He roared into the trees. Chamboko followed at a safe distance. Edmond had completely abandoned his body to his father. His easy gait had changed to a military upright dignity. His stomach bulged. The veins in his arms thickened. The king threw off the shoes on Edmond's feet and ripped off his shirt.

Chamboko picked up the shoes and the torn shirt and stuffed them into Edmond's bundle and carried it together with his own.

The king started in the direction of the mountain Chamboko had pointed to Edmond as his father's burial ground. Chamboko carried Edmond's bundle on his head and his own over his shoulder.

The king did not choose the human footpaths Chamboko and Edmond would have chosen. He walked straight through bushes and thorns on Edmond's bare feet. He whipped tree branches out of his way with the ease of brushing off tall grass aside. The sun went down and darkness fell. That did not lessen his speed. He walked through the undergrowth with authority and ignored darkness and everything else in his way.

Chamboko with the weight of two bundles on his head and shoulder was hard put to keep up. Around midnight, Chamboko called out to the king to rest Edmond's body.

"You have made my son a weakling." the king said with a voice full of anger and impatience, but he sat down. Chamboko was out of breath, he crashed onto the ground beside the king.

"You have become a weak man yourself too. See how a little walk has got you punting like a rabbit running from dogs."

"My lord, it's age. I am getting old."

"Phew! Old? Your grandfather was the strongest runner even when he was an old man. Chamboko, shape up!"

"Yes, my lord."

Chamboko was indeed very tired, but the king even in his time with his own human body was a strong man whose vigour had no equal.

The king started whistling and humming to himself ignoring the panting Chamboko. After a long while, the king stood up. "Let's go."

Chamboko succumbing to sleep, jumped to his feet and grabbed the two bundles.

"Give me that." the king said reaching for Edmond's bundle with his hand holding the musket.

"I'll carry it my lord." Chamboko protested weakly.

"Carrying bundles like women. Give it to me. Oh, my ancestors! Now Chamboko makes me a servant."

The king grabbed Edmond's bundle and started walking. Chamboko hastened to stay close to him.

All through the night, the moon had been buried behind dark clouds but now the clouds began to part for the moon. Chamboko could see better with the moonlight, but their path was no less arduous.

The king tore through bush and tree like an animal. Chamboko stayed as close as possible to avoid the whiplash of the tree branches the king parted out of his way. They walked until morning.

Although Chamboko was tired, daylight opened his eyes to familiar sights. Under the vines of the wilderness, the remnants of what was left of the king's court invigorated him. The sound of the waterfalls coming from Matonga River and the mountains bordering its valley gave him a wholesome feeling that he was now home. The mountain where he had buried the king rose clearly before him, solemn and unchanged. But now, steel beams like the ones they had just seen at BL Mines pierced the sky, a jarring intrusion on sacred ground. He hurried to catch up with the king to ask him about it, but he decided against it.

The king headed for the valley of the Matonga River. They walked until a lone hut sitting at the edge of the forest came into sight. When the king bellowed and raised his scepter and musket, Chamboko knew they had reached their destination.

"Matinenga!" the king called out. There was no reply. He sat down at the door of the hut and laid down and roared. Then suddenly, Edmond's body convulsed, and a slow whistle escaped from his lips. For the first time since he gripped the scepter, he let it go as his spirit left Edmond's body.

Chamboko sat down too and watched as Edmond's body lying before him twisted itself into a fetal position and fell asleep. He kept watching, waiting for instructions or movement from the hut. There was none. Soon, he too fell asleep.

Chapter Thirteen

Chamboko and Edmond or Edmond's body slept until Edmond himself woke up. The sun was in the same position as it had been when they had reached the cave the previous day. Edmond was surprised to find himself dressed in a leopard's skin with no shoes on. His feet were as sore as the rest of his body was. He looked around and recognized Chamboko but nothing else. He dragged himself and reached Chamboko and shook him.

"Sekuru, wake up." he said quietly. Chamboko woke up hailing the king.

"My lord, I must have fallen asleep."

"Sekuru, where are we?" Edmond asked, puzzled by the servile expression on Chamboko's face, addressing him as "My Lord".

"Oh Matonga, a wonderful thing happened. Your father came and brought us here."

"What do you mean, my father came?"

"Of course you wouldn't know Matonga. See how you're dressed? You're blessed. The kings' spirit came and possessed you."

"What?"

"That mark in your left palm was made by that walking stick there," he said indicating the scepter that was lying beside the musket. "It's a royal scepter. Do not touch it with your left hand, the king will come through you if you do." Chamboko said with reverence in his voice.

Edmond gazed at the scepter, once it had been no more than a decorated walking stick in his eyes. But something in Chamboko's voice silenced all doubt. The last thing he remembered from the cave was the strange pull - the compulsion to reach out and touch it. After that he had no recollection of the overnight journey that had brought them to the hut.

Edmond's mind was lost trying to piece together the events that had brought them to the hut when he heard Chamboko enthusiastically say, "Oh yes, the ancestors have come upon us and you are their mouthpiece."

Edmond had no idea what Chamboko was talking about. Of course, he knew about magic and sorcery, but this felt different. It wasn't a spell. It was his father speaking through him. He didn't understand it. Not fully. But he liked the idea. For the first time in his life, he didn't feel like an orphan, a child adrift in the world. He had grown up being told by his mother and Chamboko that his father would live through him; that was comforting. However, now that he knew it was real filled him with a joy that surpassed everything he'd ever known.

"What did the king say? When did he come? When did he leave?" Edmond fired the questions rapidly.

"He hasn't spoken yet. The only thing he wanted was vaMatinenga."

"VaMatinenga?" Edmond knew who she was, but nothing made sense to him then.

"Yes."

Consciousness of where they were was beginning to dawn on him. The hut with its closed door drew his attention.

"What's in there." he asked pointing at the door.

"I don't know."

"What do we do now?"

"We wait I am sure the king will return soon."

"Do you think there's someone in there?"

"Maybe."

"Isn't this the place where the *baas boy* said we would find the old woman?"

"I think so."

"If my father was calling vaMatinenga, don't you think he was referring to her." He said pointing at the door.

"Ah Matonga, the ways of the ancestors are strange. It could be her, but it has been twenty years. I didn't think there would be anyone left here."

The knowledge that he had carried the spirit of his father gave him the confidence to get up and investigate the hut. He knocked on the door. There was no answer. He pushed it open and saw a human form lying on a reed mat under the cover of an antelope blanket. He closed the door and went back to Chamboko.

"There's someone in there."

"There is? What are they doing?"

"I don't know, the person may not even be alive."

"Let's leave it alone Matonga. We will find out soon enough."

That satisfied Edmond.

"I am hungry sekuru, can we get something to eat?"

"I had forgotten about the food myself. We haven't eaten in the two days you know". Chamboko stood up and stretched.

"I'll light a fire over there."

"No, no Matonga, rest, I'll do it." Chamboko said thinking how tired Edmond must be from the hike his father had subjected his body to.

Edmond opened his eyes and ears to the country around him for the first time. The distant sounds of the waterfalls on the river played music to his ears. The green wilderness that stopped at the edge of the forest where the hut was, was richer than any he had seen on their journey. The valley that flowed from the forest sweeping down towards what he imagined was the river was breath taking. The mountains that had once looked so distant and beyond reach towered above the valley like fortifications for a garden made for his pleasure. The richness of the panorama was an opiate to his tired mind.

Slowly, he drifted back to sleep; and in sleep, he dreamed. He dreamed of a long time before his birth, a distant age where he was alive, not as himself, but as his father. In the dream, he soared like a bird over the kingdom, watching over the land and its people. He was a great man, his heart vast, full of life. He was the messenger of Matonga, the sacred link between the people and the Creator. Faces he had never seen before filled the valley below, countless and waiting, all of them looking to him for a word.

Chamboko woke him up to eat.

They ate in silence occasionally staring at the door of the hut. Chamboko was on edge paying attention to Edmond in anticipation of the return of the king. But the king did not return, then.

They finished eating and decided to tour the valley and have a drink of water at the river. Edmond put on his shoes and recovered his torn shirt from his bundle and followed Chamboko.

An overwhelming sense of wellbeing flowed through Edmond's blood as he looked at the endless valley. The knowledge that this was all his ancestors' land infused richness in the ground, the grass and the trees. His high spirits touched all around him and made him light on his feet. They walked across the valley to the river.

"This is Matonga River. The lifeblood of your people." Chamboko said pointing at the river whose width dominated the valley."

"Where does it start from?"

"In the land of Kaonde in the hills far, far away from here."

"And the waterfalls, where are they?"

"It's too far for us to walk there. It took the king and I two months to walk there."

"But they sound like they are just around the bend."

"That's because they are huge. The water falls from a height six times the height of a man standing."

"I want to see them one day."

"After we get settled and build ourselves places to sleep, we'll go there."

"I didn't mean now."

"I know, I know, just thinking ahead." Chamboko spoke merrily, happy that Edmond seemed to have completely bought into settling here to start rebuilding Matonganyika.

They were at the beginning of the banks of the river. Reeds and water flows formed a broad lining cutting off the valley. Edmond turned and admired the valley. It inclined from the riverbanks carrying a green carpet of long-stemmed crawling grass that blanketed everything up to the forest. On the other side of the river, the banks were the same and the valley continued outward on treeless ground. It stretched to the river at the bottom of the mountains.

Chamboko led Edmond to a rock that sat on their side of the riverbank like a springboard. On its sides were a series of smaller rocks with heads sticking out of the flowing but peaceful river.

They decided to wash themselves.

"Where did you bury my father?" Edmond asked looking at the mountains across

"You can't see the place from here."

"Is it far?"

"No."

"Can you take me there?"

"That's what we came here for Matonga. The more you see of your people the better you'll be prepared for the work ahead of us." Chamboko said drying himself with his shirt.

They dressed and went up stream to an old rickety makeshift bridge fashioned with loosely strung together logs whose survival had clearly defied time. Gingerly, they trapezed on the logs and crossed the river. Chamboko was familiar with every nook and cranny at the bottom of the mountains.

"The king used to sit up here watching the races." Chamboko

said pointing to a ledge above them.

"What races?"

"Didn't I tell you about the races. As a matter of fact, the king reminded me of my grandfather's prowess."

"What are you talking about?"

"Every summer after the harvest, all the runners from here to Kaonde came to compete.

Their course was the length of the valley, up and down and the winner was the first person to cross that bridge we crossed on."

"That death trap?" Edmond asked aghast that anyone would risk their life by running across what looked like a makeshift bridge.

"Matonga, it looks unstable now, but in its time it could hold the weight of a bull." Chamboko insisted, "It did. The king slaughtered a small herd of cattle in honour of the winner, and my grandfather got the honour until he died."

Chamboko chuckled which sent Edmond into laughter.

Chamboko found the trail leading up the mountain. It was a path going around rocks and trees and wide enough for both to walk abreast of each other.

"What did you use this trail for?" Edmond asked.

"To go up the mountain."

"I can see that sekuru. What I mean is, why is it so wide?"

"A lot of ceremonies were held up here. The trail just grew from use."

"Oh."

As they climbed, Chamboko noticed rocks that did not blend with the staid picture of the mountain. There were broken tree branches on the ground and the vegetation was generally disturbed. Edmond noticed it too but did not comment.

When they reached the place, Chamboko found the answer to the puzzle. The ground had been leveled and cleared of all vegetation. Steel beams like the ones they had seen at the mine fisted the air. Chamboko just stood and stared flabbergasted by the sight before him.

"Could I be wrong?" Chamboko wondered out loud.

"What?"

"This is the king's burial ground, at least that's what I thought." he looked around him. "His father is buried on his own mountain yonder and his own in another. This mountain is the Lion king's burial ground and yet all I see is the cleared ground."

Hesitantly he led Edmond on a search which he hoped would end in a mistake - that they were on the wrong mountain. But it was no mistake. They approached a long steel beam that stood in the middle of the mountain. Another that looked like it, but with a top holding a cross member of what seemed to be a pulley, was deep in a hole in the ground. They peered into the hole. The broken clay pot they had used to carry the token possessions of the deceased gaped at them; a moth eaten black and white shroud covered the base of the hole. Sand had fallen in but a gold bangle and copper bracelet protruded under it.

"Oh, my ancestors!" Chamboko swore under his breath.

"What is it?"

"They have desecrated the king's grave."

"Is this it?"

"My ancestors, yes." Chamboko answered with tears forming in his eyes.

From nowhere appeared the huge lion they had encountered in the enchanted forest. It roared and roared and sauntered towards them. Edmond's initial reaction was to run, but Chamboko held his hand. They sat down and chanted to the roar of the lion.

"Matonga, my Lord. We have come back to pay our respects. We are your children."

The lion came closer and sat by the grave side across from where they were sitting its eyes, as before, did not leave theirs. No longer afraid, a sense of profound sadness and compassion overwhelmed Edmond as he looked at the beast. Tears flowed down his face. The countenance of the lion was ferocious, yet all fear left Edmond. He saw age and helplessness in its fiery eyes. He was no longer looking at a strange vicious beast of the jungle but his own father. He felt as close to the animal as he could have ever felt for his father had he ever met him in the flesh. The sorrow that he saw before him and the emptiness of the hole below him, made him clap his hands in prayer with a wordless promise that he would do every bidding his father commanded. The lion seemed to have heard Edmond's unspoken promise. It roared, stood on its feet and sauntered off, disappearing as suddenly as it appeared.

When the lion was gone, Chamboko related the anger he had heard in the king's voice when he had possessed Edmond's body in the cave. Edmond now understood it all and asked no questions.

After Chamboko's explanation, Edmond had no more interest in the mountains and the land below. The magic was gone.

Chapter 14

They climbed down the mountain and crossed the river in silence. As they approached the perimeter of the hut, they saw a human figure open the door and slip inside. The figure's back, draped in an antelope-fur blanket, was so bent that without the cane supporting them they might have fallen headfirst to the ground. Their glimpse was so brief that neither Edmond nor Chamboko had time to call out a greeting.

"I think that was the person I saw lying on the floor when I opened the door." Edmond whispered.

"Maybe… if that's vaMatinenga, she must be over a hundred years old." Chamboko said

"But my father has only been dead twenty years..."

"She was older than your father. She was bequeathed to him at birth long before your father was born."

A rush of questions swamped Edmond's mind, but he never got a chance to ask any of them. A voice, as loud as day, commanded them to enter the hut. They clapped their hands at the door and asked for permission to enter. It was granted.

They entered the hut. Though the fireplace held no flame and no other light source was visible, a dim luminescence and gentle warmth filled the space. Edmond, seated on the floor beside Chamboko, studied the old woman wrapped in antelope fur. Her face was sculpted with thick ridges of wrinkles, and though her eyes seemed open, he was not sure. Even if they were, the folds of aged flesh above her brows appeared to narrow her vision. However, Edmond sensed she had no need for sight she saw everything without it. Beside the reed mat she sat on stood two clay pots adorned with beads of red, black, and white. In her right hand she held a tiny gourd closed with a piece of wood; her left gripped a cane that helped her sit upright. With a slow motion, she pushed the fur blanket behind her, revealing a smooth, bald head.

She coughed and opened her gourd with one hand and sat it down.

Gripping the cane with her underarm, she forced a tiny pinch of snuff tobacco from the gourd into her open palm. She raised her palm to her nose and snorted the snuff out of it. When the snuff took effect, she sneezed.

"Our Queen Mother! We hear you!" Chamboko and Edmond shouted in response to the sneeze. The small old woman straightened up with a quickness that belied her age.

"Do you know who I am? uhm?" she challenged them with a loud manly voice.

"Do you know me?" she challenged again.

"No, but we know you are our mother, Your Highness." Chamboko replied nudging Edmond to clap his hand in unison.

"Why did you bring my husband here, you fool?" the woman demanded.

"I don't understand." Chamboko said.

"Why did you bring my husband here? Wasn't I fighting well and good, alone?" her eyes, which could barely see, glared at them.

That question was the last thing Edmond heard. He suddenly scrambled out of the hut and immediately scrambled back inside with the scepter and musket which were on the ground just outside at the door. The scepter was in his left hand and the musket in his right hand.

The body belonged to Edmond, but it was the king taking over.

Brandishing the scepter he declared, "I am here." It was not Edmond's voice.   King Chokwedu was back in Edmond's body.

"I am here!" declared the king again.

Chamboko clapped his hands.

The king, in Edmond's body, strutted about dominating the hut.

Edmond's body suddenly grew bigger and stood straight up, his head towering into the roof. Finally, he sat down opposite the old woman.

"Chamboko, did you see what they did to me? Did you see?"

"Yes, My Lord." Chamboko said, surmising that the king was talking about his violated grave.

"Iwe *(hey you)* Chamboko!" the ageless woman's voice leapt at him, sharp and sudden. "Now that you've brought my husband's son here, where is your army? Where are your weapons?"

Chamboko flinched. "I don't understand, Your Highness," he said meekly.

"No, you wouldn't, would you?" she snapped. "Did you not understand the Lion, the king himself, blocking your path, warning you not to bring his son here?"

She paused to hear what he had to say, but Chamboko did not have anything to say.

"This boy is our only son. Did you not see that he did not want to return? We did not summon him. This was all your idea."

Chamboko pleaded, "I thought it was the wish of the ancestors… now that he has some money to marry and restock the cattle."

She scoffed. "You think and speak like a child. Where is the land to restock on? Did the enemy feasting on my husband's soil give you permission to reclaim it without a fight?" she paused and continued. "You talk about money. What money? Do you think the scraps he earns from the yellow-bearded men are enough to restore Matonganyika?"

"I thought he wanted to come back," Chamboko said, his voice faltering.

"Come back to do what?" she barked. "You call yourself a man, yet you don't even carry a walking stick!"

Her voice rose, fierce and unrelenting.

"Did you take this boy to the hill where the half-burnt log of the ancestors lies? Did you kindle its flame?"

"No, Queen Mother," Chamboko answered, sheepish and ashamed.

"So, you expect this boy to fight for his father with bare hands, without the blessing of the ancestors?"

Chamboko had no answer. None was expected. He was a servant. Servants do not talk back to their master.

She continued, her voice now a storm: "When we let you take our son to your homeland, you knew what you were leaving behind. You left this land knowing the enemy had vanquished Matonganyika. There was nothing left. Only my sisters and I remained, to stand beside the king. We stayed. And now, all my sisters have perished. I am alone. I live by the will of the Creator to defend my husband's legacy and honour. Had it not been for the strength of my husband and the power of my father's ancestors, I too would have perished. I have defended this land, this land of Matonganyika, alone. I do not need your false promises. My husband's spirit is troubled enough without you bringing his son, the future leader of Matonga clan here unprepared, to be devoured by yellow-bearded men."

vaMatinenga spoke with a voice far larger than her frail, shrunken body. Her words carried power; power that shook Chamboko to his core. All Chamboko could do was look down on the floor with nothing to say.

"I will fight!" the king shouted.

"With what?" vaMatinenga challenged.

"I will fight!" the king repeated.

They fell silent.

"Matonga, my lord," vaMatinenga said in a conciliatory voice, "I know you will fight. You died fighting but is this the time? Have you organized...?"

"You haven't seen my fire? You haven't seen my mist? Haven't you seen me? I am the lion!"

"Yes, we have seen it. But the son whose body you now inhabit is still young, and he stands alone. As King Chokwedu, you forged coalitions with every neighbour; none of them are here. The few Matonga clansmen who escaped the war of the yellow-bearded men are scattered across unknown lands. Have you gathered them back already? Great king, you cannot face this enemy by yourself. And first, your son must climb the Hill of the Half-Burnt Log and kindle the flame: a task you cannot perform, for you are now a spirit."

"I fought alone."

"I honour you, my Lord. But you yourself admitted on the mountain of refuge: we lost the war because we did not climb the hill, we did not kindle the flame, and so the ancestors could not advise or intervene…"

"I know that! I made a mistake - one I am still paying for."

"Only the living may climb the hill and lay the request before the Council of the Ancestors, the very council you will join when you choose to depart and take your place among them."

"I am the Lion. I am King Chokwedu. I will not flee to the Council until I have corrected the mistake that cost me my kingdom."

Chamboko sat quietly, as was expected of servants, listening to the exchange between the ageless queen and her dead husband. She was so old she might have been mistaken for the dead herself, and he, the proud king with a restless spirit, was no longer flesh. Together, they made a married couple like no other. Chamboko had nothing to contribute: he had stumbled into a realm where mere mortals were no more relevant than the floor he sat on.

"Matonga, my lord," vaMatinenga implored, her voice trembling with urgency. "Send this man back. You have blessed your son well. Give him time to grow before asking him to stand in your place. You can see he carries a great future. Through this boy, in time, your grandchildren and their children and Matonga clansmen scattered in faraway places shall come together and restore Matonganyika to its glory."

The king did not respond. But the silence spoke. He knew she was right. This was not the time.

vaMatinenga pressed on, filling the silence with memory and prophecy.

"Prince Zharara, who became King Zharara, your great-great-great ancestor, did not build Matonganyika alone. The yellow-bearded men are not gods. They just caught you unprepared because you had not climbed the hill to the fire of the half-burnt log of the ancestors. It is well known here in the realm of the air; you shall conquer them and reclaim your glory. But only if you wait and follow the footsteps of the great Zharara."

The king's voice cracked through the silence.

"I exist in no man's land- a purgatory between worlds. I cannot take my rightful seat among the ancestors because my life was left unfinished, cut short in a manner worse than that of an animal… never mind a man of royal blood. I accept that, as a man, I was defeated by other men. Such things happen in the world of flesh; they happened even in my father's time. But how can I rise and take my place as an ancestor when we all know my death was unnatural? I was strung from a tree like a useless cow. Tell me - where in the history of our people who came from the river in the north where life begins was any man, let alone a king, ever hung from a tree? It is unconscionable. They killed me, insulted me, and seized Matonganyika, my kingdom. And as if that were not enough, they opened my grave to the jackals of the jungle."

"I have your body with me," vaMatinenga said softly. She reached into a clay pot and lifted a human bone, skeletal remains of the king himself.

"You see that?" he growled. "While my forefathers lie in peace, my spirit roams these yellow bearded men's mine sand dunes in my valley with what is left of my earthly remains protected by a woman…"

"Matonga. Great Lion," she said, her voice steady. "We live together. You and my ancestors protect me. I have no power to shield one as great as you. I beg you, let your son return to live and learn the ways and the sorcery of the yellow-bearded men for himself. So, he can learn to use their own sorcery on them."

She clapped her feeble hands in supplication.

"You know it is as certain as the words I speak. Matonganyika shall be restored through your son and his children, as your ancestors in Rimuka, in the valley of the river in the north where the world begins, ordained it. Your grandchildren will rise, using the yellow bearded men's own sorcery and children and defeat the yellow-bearded men and drive them from your kingdom. No one knows your pain more deeply than I do. But let him return, my lord. Through this boy, you shall live forever. You shall reign again, through all eternity."

The king was pacified.

He began to whistle his favorite song. The queen joined him.

"The trees bow down to the wind... The grass bows down to the elephant... Our lord bows down to no one….."

Chamboko clapped his hands in rhythm, the song stirring memories deep in his bones. They sang the chorus of songs from the past, one leading into another-songs that recalled the great days when Matonganyika was paradise, when God, the ancestors, and man walked as one. Chamboko knew them all.

Eventually the king stopped singing and broke into a hearty laugh.

"I am greatness itself." he declared jovially, "I fear no man. It is only a matter of time before the flame of the half-burnt log of my ancestors burns bright again. I shall wait. My land, I shall reclaim one day. The world shall no longer laugh at me as the king who lost Matonganyika to the yellow bearded men."

"We hear you, Great King." Chamboko praised.

"Before you return, I want you to take my son back to my house. Help him fill it with the granite rocks of our land. Put a marker to let the world know what is there before I pounce on them. Let him know the future is good, and that I will be with him always. Tell him to learn the ways of the yellow bearded men but never divulge the location of the hill of the half-burnt log which I shall show him in time." the king instructed.

"It will be done," Chamboko said quietly. With that assurance, the king laid Edmond's body down and left it.

Edmond's body rocked and twisted as the king's spirit stretched out from within him. All the while, Chamboko and the ageless queen clapped their hands, singing praises to the king, bidding him farewell.

When the spirit finally departed, Edmond lay flat on his back, as if in a deep sleep.

"You will leave with our prince immediately," the old queen said. "This land is a battleground. Staying here would only waste the prince's life."

"Begging your pardon, Your Highness, but where shall we go?" Chamboko asked earnestly, because in truth, he dreaded returning to Chikwepa's farm. Even without title to the land, being in Matonganyika felt more honourable than living out there.

"What kind of fool are you?" she snapped. "Where shall you go? Did you burn the home you've been living in when you began this journey?"

"No, Your Highness."

"Then why speak like a child? You will return to where you came from. The spirits of the ancestors tried to warn you, but you would not listen. It still puzzles my old mind why you brought Tarwa here. It was nothing but foolishness."

"He wanted to see his land," Chamboko murmured.

"I understand. And I do thank you for the good work you've done with our son. But he is still young. His land will always be here, it is not going anywhere. Please lead him back to where you came from. Do you understand me?"

"Yes, Your Highness."

"At first light, go. Do as the king commanded, and leave."

"Yes, Your Highness."

"Bid the prince farewell for me. I have things to do for my husband."

With those words, she set down her cane. She heaved a long sigh, as if breathing out the last of her strength. She pulled the antelope fur blanket over herself and became the curled and gnarled figure they had seen lying on that reed mat when they arrived.

The small hut suddenly felt vast, an empty dome echoing with silence. Chamboko was left in a great expanse of loneliness. Edmond, his body exhausted by the spirit of the late king, remained in deep sleep. vaMatinenga, more dead than alive, was dead, for now.

A chill ran down Chamboko's spine. He felt like a man sitting among the dead. The emptiness of the hut and the loneliness pressing in on him forced his mind back over the events of the day, and over his own life. Twenty years had passed since his days in the king's court had ended, and now, after travelling a full circle to reclaim that life, he saw the truth: there was nothing left in the past he had come searching for. He had never accepted the life he lived in Chiweshe. His will to go on had rested on one belief, that it was temporary, that he would return to Matonganyika. But now he had returned, and the past had closed its doors to him. He was a man with nothing to show for the only time his life had ever meant anything. His future was the present: a cold expanse of loneliness in which he neither belonged nor wished to belong. If vaMatinenga would only let him stay with her, his life might still hold a semblance of meaning. But she had closed that door too.

Edmond had his life in the white man's town, where he no longer needed Chamboko. Even Chikwepa's farm, of all places, had no use for him either.

That was his present. That was his future.

He stretched himself on the floor to sleep but could not. There was no space for him in vaMatinenga's hut nor in the world he tried to re-enter.

He rose and stepped outside.

Chapter 15

Although it was late in the night, that did not register in Chamboko's mind. He could not sleep anyway. The warm air under the bright moon and stars was a welcome tonic after the coldness of the hut. He found himself walking towards Matonga River. He made his way easily through the makeshift bridge. He stopped on the other side and sat down. While his mind rested in serenity the river gave the valley, his body was on edge. Abruptly he stood up and followed the trail up the mountain until he reached the empty grave. Then, the mission on his mind came into focus. He was going to fill the grave as the king had ordered. He looked around the grave site. There were no rocks anywhere in sight.

Remembering the rocks he had seen at the bottom of the mountain, he followed the trail down until he found sizable rocks. He lined them up and began hurling them up the mountain with nothing on his mind.

Edmond woke up at daybreak. He found himself alone. vaMatinenga was still dead to the world tucked under the complete cover of the antelope fur. His body weighed like an elephant and ached with every beat of his heart. He found his torn shirt beside him and put it on out of habit. Gingerly, he stood and wobbled his way outside the hut looking for Chamboko. He was nowhere in sight, but a track of his footsteps was clear in the dew laden grass.

He followed the track. It soon disappeared but he decided to continue to the river to refresh his weary body. He dipped himself in the cool clear water. It was good. It numbed some of the aches and reinvigorated him. As he dried himself with his tattered shirt, he saw Chamboko in the distance hurling a heavy rock up the mountain. He shouted and waved to him. Chamboko called back and waved him over with his free hand. Edmond slipped into his trousers and crossed the river to join Chamboko. Chamboko was draped in perspiration resting on the rock he had been carrying.

He smiled as Edmond approached and waved him to sit down. He wasted no time. He told Edmond all that had transpired since he had been possessed by the king's spirit and the king's orders. As soon as he finished, Edmond stood up ready to join Chamboko to complete their task.

With four hands doing the work, they soon had the grave filled with rocks. On Edmond's suggestion, they pulled down the steel beam that stood beside the grave. It came down and tumbled to the bottom of the mountain. Then they built a stone enclosure around the grave. When their task was completed, they sat down and rededicated the grave to their ancestors.

Edmond knew, even without Chamboko explaining much, that they were going back to Chiweshe. He seemed detached from it all, it did not really matter anymore. He had lost the desperate urgency he'd felt when his life had seemed threatened in the wilderness. He was in the land of Matonga. He had reached Matonganyika and walked its soil. But there was no elation in that fact anymore. It was as if the land were not there at all. He had made the journey, but he had not found what he was looking for. All he had found was mining machinery, gorging up everything, even the sacred grave of his father.

&

vaMatinenga slept all day, every day.

Edmond and Chamboko made a fire outside and roasted the last of their meat provision.

"Sekuru, what does she live on?" Edmond asked, chewing a piece of meat pointing to the door where vaMatinenga slept.

"Eh, I don't know, Matonga. I was thinking we could stay here and help her with food but… eh, she told us to leave," Chamboko said

119

ruefully, already thinking of the bleak prospects ahead.

"Is that what she said?"

"Yes."

"And my father, what did he say?"

"The same. There is nothing for us here. Not now, anyway."

"What do you mean, *not now anyway?*"

"The king said he will guide you. He will bring you back here when the time comes to reclaim the land. He said he will lead you to the hill of the half-burnt log, where you shall meet the ancestors for guidance."

"Where is that hill?"

"I do not know. In the king's time we never went there, so I do not know where it is."

"So… we are going back? But we are already here."

Chamboko's responses to Edmond's questions were dry. There was a future; yes, a future for Edmond. But Chamboko saw none for himself in any of it. There was no timeline, no certainty. Edmond was young; he had time. Chamboko felt that whatever future was coming would not arrive in his own lifetime.

Although Edmond had already sensed it, he did not find any logic to it. He wanted to ask Chamboko to recount to him again everything that had transpired and what had been said that made their return to Chiweshe so resolute, but the sadness in Chamboko's face stopped him. Like Chamboko he felt so sad and empty that tears fell down his eyes.

Chamboko cried with him. They mourned the death of their lives, the dream that had bonded them together. Their future hung in the blindness of the dark night their tomorrow, and all the days ahead, portended to be.

They spent a fortnight hunting the plentiful deer that came to the river. They brought the deer to the hut, skinned them and stored the venison both for vaMatinenga and for themselves for their journey. They spent their nights under the stars talking and slept by the fire they kept going beside the hut. In all that time, they never saw vaMatinenga get up. Edmond looked in on her every morning and afternoon and always found her in the same position under the antelope fur blanket. Reluctantly, they made plans for the journey ahead and decided to return to the mining compound and see if they could not find a lift going in the direction of Salisbury.

In the dawn of the morning of their departure, they went into the hut and sat down. They clapped their hands and bade vaMatinenga farewell. She did not respond. It was as if they were talking to a dead body. They gathered their bundles and left.

They went back via the cave at the former trading post - hunting lodge. The wilderness held no threat to Edmond anymore. He walked confidently sensing the spirit of his father hovering above, everywhere in the forest, looking after him.

By nightfall, they reached the cave. Edmond, using his right hand with deliberate care, returned the royal scepter and musket to their place on the wall. They spent the night there in silence.

In the morning, Edmond surveyed the treasures of cave with a newfound sense of ownership, one he hadn't felt when they first arrived. From a rock shelf, he took a pouch made of elephant hide and filled it with gold ingots and coins from the broken clay pot. He weighed the idea of taking more, then quietly let it go.

"What should we do to conceal the cave?" he asked Chamboko.

Chamboko smiled. "The Lion knows better than we ever will, how to guard its treasures. The Lion is always watching. We have nothing to hide."

Chamboko added, "Whoever has the *misfortune* of entering this place without permission will never leave the cave with anything, maybe, not even his life."

That satisfied Edmond. He had seen the power of the ancestors for himself. They left the cave as they had found it and headed to the mining compound.

The *baas boy* was happy to see them back. To the *baas boy*, Chamboko and Edmond, were two able bodied men he was going to take to his bosses to be hired as mine-labourers. As he explained, the mine was in constant need of labour because many left as soon as they learnt of the strange occurrences that dogged the land. The *baas boy* offered Chamboko and Edmond the jobs in the evening when they were preparing to sleep.

Chamboko thought about it and liked the idea. Working in the mines in the land that had held everything that had been his life seemed like a good compromise.

But Edmond was deeply offended by the offer.

"Do I look like a mindless rabbit that burrows the soil it feeds on? This is my land, and I will die first before I work with the people who hung my father to take it and make dust heaps out of it." He declared and stormed out of the hut.

Although his outburst caught Chamboko by surprise, it also presented him with a new man. He admired the anger and pride he saw in Edmond.

The *baas boy* was bewildered; all he had done was offer them employment as he did with everyone he met.

Left alone with Chamboko, he listened as Chamboko recounted all that had happened since they had left the mine including the restoration of the king's grave they had done.

The confusion on the *baas boy's* face slowly turned to understanding.

He went outside and found Edmond. "Matonga, I am sorry for all that has happened," he said.

"It's not your fault, there is nothing to forgive," Edmond responded detecting the respect in the *baas boy's* voice. They talked, Edmond with authority and the *baas boy* with the servility of one standing in another's house. When they went back inside the *baas boy* had another idea.

"Would you be willing to come with me in the morning to see my white men and tell them about the king's grave"? he asked. "I think it is best they know the wrongs they have done your ancestors."

"But that won't stop them from mining, will it?" asked Edmond.

"I do not think so Matonga. They say the money they make out of these mines is worth more than what they make anywhere else where they are mining."

"Then I do not see the point. If you can only help us, find a lift back to Salisbury, we will leave you alone with your mines. My ancestors can deal with this better than I can."

"Salisbury is more than five hundred miles away and there is no motorcar that goes there unless the white man has deliveries to make."

"How often is that?"

"Oh, once every three months."

"When was the last delivery?"

The *baas boy* thought for a moment and answered, "A week before you arrived here the first time."

Edmond had no idea what five hundred miles meant, all he knew was that Harare was far, far, away. He mauled over the fact that there would be no motorcars going in that direction for two months. He was no longer afraid of the wild forest they had traveled through on foot. He concluded that he was willing to walk back even if it took him the rest of his life. Chamboko did not say anything. He had resigned himself to doing whatever Edmond decided. They went to sleep without any resolution.

The *baas boy* left them in his hut in the morning when he went on his shift and told them to feel at home. He came back in the middle of his shift accompanied by two white men, the shift foreman, and the head white man, the manager of the mine.

Chamboko was frightened when they were introduced by the *baas boy* to the white man. Edmond had no such fear.

"How are you, please, baas" he greeted the white men.

The *baas boy* explained to Chamboko and Edmond that he had told the white men what they had told him.

The foreman spoke a mixture of English and local languages. He was familiar with the reverence Africans placed on their ancestors.

The two white men had been at the mines long enough to know that the disasters that had befallen the mines, the inexplicable fires, mist, the lion and the old woman were supernatural. They had asked the *baas boy* to bring them to Edmond and Chamboko so that they could hear the history behind it for themselves.

In the past, it would have been Chamboko who spoke. But now, Edmond stepped forward naturally. With quiet confidence, he used his broken English and native tongues to tell the story of his people, the Matonga, and the kingdom beneath their feet, Matonganyika.

He spoke of generations past, from Prince Zharara to his own father. He described the peace that once reigned across the region, stretching from the mountains to the ocean. As he recounted his father's rule, his voice sharpened, echoing the anger and pride of the man who had birthed him.

He told of the war that shattered the region, a war that offered no peace, not even to those who surrendered. He described their flight into the mountains, the surrender, and his father's hanging. He spoke of Chamboko and his mother's long trek to Chiweshe, her death, and his own journey to Salisbury. He spoke of Mr. Jim, of labour, of return, of the mine, of vaMatinenga and of the desecration of his father's grave.

When he finished, his eyes burned red with tears of rage.

They all sat in silence, with obvious respect for the young man who had addressed them.

"What can we do? We cannot rewind the clock of history. We are only employees of the B.L. Mining Company. The people whose arms your father fought run the government. The mining Company only bought the land from the government." the head white man spoke.

"What I would ask, if I could ask, you cannot give me. As I told your *baas boy* there's nothing I can do, the ancestors will do what they will." Edmond said with finality.

"But we can at least show respect for the late great king and give him his due respect and consecrate his grave." the *baas boy* said.

"Well spoken," the foreman said. He turned to his boss, "You know, these things happen all the time and I have often thought about it. I remember down in South Africa; we had a problem similar to B.L.'s and the mining company did exactly like he is saying."

"Why didn't you suggest it before?"

"How could I? I had no knowledge of the history of the people."

"I am a Christian but wasn't it Jesus, who said, "Render to Caesar the things that belong to Caesar?" the mine manager responded.

"Yes."

The head white man spoke to Edmond in *Chilapalapa* and asked him to help them honour his ancestors and their land. Edmond related it to Chamboko, and the old man readily agreed. But Edmond surprised him with his newfound confidence and wisdom again.

He said, "It is not my place, or anyone present here to speak for my ancestors or my father. I will have to consult them before I agree to participate in anything you may want to do."

His answer was received with respect. The two white men said they would wait to hear from him and left.

"Matonga, forgive me, I spoke before thinking. You are correct, the decision rests not with us but with the owners of the land."

Chamboko apologized after the white men and the *baas boy* left.

"Sekuru, nothing we say and do matters, the problem is too big for mere mortals like you and I to solve."

"But we can try,"

"Yes, I think we can." After a moment's reflections, Edmond continued, "The only thing to do is to return to vaMatinenga and ask for her advice."

"Well said. Yes, she is the only one who can tell us what to do."

"But supposing she doesn't want to talk to us."

"She will, this is important. The land and your father's spirit are the only two things she lives for."

The whistle marking the end of the first shift blew and the mine labourers trooped out making way for the second shift.

The *baas boy* found Edmond and Chamboko preparing to leave to go and consult vaMatinenga.

"Can I accompany you" the *baas boy* asked eagerly.

"What about your work." Edmond responded.

"Hah, this is my work. If these mines shut down, what work do I have?"

"I see, you want to come and speak on behalf of the white men?", Chamboko asked.

"Yes."

&

Accompanied by the *baas boy* they left that afternoon and arrived at their destination around the same time the next day. The sight that greeted them was spectacular. vaMatinenga in fine regalia was sitting outside her hut.

She wore a fur hat to match the quilt covering her body.

It seemed as if the multi-coloured quilt covering her body was made of all the animals of the earth. Gold and bead bracelets shined on her wrists and ankles. She was not the same person they had left lying comatose.

They approached cautiously.

"Matonga, you are back," vaMatinenga greeted them.

Edmond and Chamboko froze. The voice was unmistakable. It was not vaMatinenga's voice. It was the voice of Edmond's late mother, vaMarunjeya. The body before them was younger, vibrant. The scraggy frame of the old, ageless woman had transformed into a radiant figure, alive and beautiful, as if time itself had bent to her spirit.

Edmond was speechless, but after all that had unfolded in the past few days, he took it in stride.

"*Hongu, amai.* We are back," he stammered, his eyes meeting hers.

They all sat down and clapped their hands in greeting.

"How have you been, Matonga? Eh, Chamboko, how are you?",

128

"We are all well if you are well, your highness, and you?"

"We are well",

"And how are they, where you are?" Chamboko added asking about the spirits of the family realizing that vaMarunjeya had possessed vaMatinenga's body.

"We are all well. Eh, Tarwa look at you, you do not eat properly do you, Matonga? "Look how skinny you are?" she asked fussing over her son.

The presence in her voice as she asked the question, overwhelmed Edmond. This was truly his mother talking to him. He smiled. She laughed.

"It is such a blessing to have you men around."

They all snickered uncertain of the meaning in her words.

"We are all very grateful for all the work you did and the meat you left us. The king was so happy with his new house on the mountain. He brought me these," she said indication the multi-coloured cover on her body. The new house on the mountain was the grave they had rebuilt for the king.

"We did not do much, amai but we are happy to know the king is pleased with our work." Chamboko said.

"I would cook for you but, these old bones can hardly move.", she said smiling with her toothless gums.

"Don't worry yourself amai, we are not hungry."

"Nonsense. Matonga, a king must always see that his people are fed. You have company let us feed them. If you don't, all the meat you left will go to waste. We have nothing but gums, we have no teeth, as you can see.", with those words she rose and stood upright like an old little girl. She did not need her cane nor was her back as bent as it had been when they first saw her. Edmond and Chamboko gawked at the wonderful sight she made.

She went inside and returned with meat, honey and fruits. She put them on the ground and sat back on the reed mat.

She hesitated as she opened her mouth unsure if she wanted to hear the answer to the question she was about to ask. "Forgive my eyes that see so falsely, but who is this man you brought with you?", she asked looking at the *baas boy*.

Chamboko cleared his throat to answer but thought better. He let Edmond speak.

"Mai Matonga, this is the head African at the diggings, he asked to come with us to see you."

They could all see that she was visibly disturbed but turned her attention away from the *baas boy* back to her son.

Deliberately keeping her focus on Edmond, she said "*Humbarume*, (gentlemen) help yourselves to the food."

They roasted the meat and ate the fruits with honey. vaMarunjeya did not look at the *baas boy* again. She devoted all her attention to her son, of whom she was obviously proud. Chamboko nudged Edmond to tell her of their mission. When he did, her head shook violently, and the body went into convulsions.

Different voices struggled to dominate her voice until vaMarunjeya, the oldest, asserted her authority as the owner of the body.

"Who is this dog you bring to our sight?" she challenged poised to jump at the *baas boy* who was caught with a chunk of meat in his throat.

"He comes in peace Mai Matonga." Chamboko pleaded.

"What does he want? I will knock his head off."

"Mai Matonga, he comes in peace. Please give us a moment to explain." Edmond said moving closer to her.

"What explanation? We know him. He has been here before. There is nothing to explain. The king told us to watch out for this snake. Get him out of my sight!" she jumped and dashed into the hut. She swiftly came back out. They did not see the spears in her hand until one swooshed past the *baas boy's* head, grazing his head. As she stooped to pick up another, Chamboko jumped to his feet and grabbed her hand. She was much, much stronger than he was but she let him take the spear.

The *baas boy* laid on the ground groaning, yelling out his innocence and covering his bleeding head with both his hands. Filled with rage, vaMatinenga turned away from them and pushed her way through the thick underbrush heading toward the river. She was gone for a while, but when she returned her anger had visibly subsided. She sat down and took a pinch of snuff to her nose.

"Speak, what do you want?" she commanded the *baas boy*.

"I beg, your pardon your highness.", the *baas boy* stammered.

"Don't ask for my pardon because you won't get it. I know why you are here. You are like a python that mesmerizes the gazelle with its slick shining skin before opening its foul mouth and devouring the poor animal. I am not a fool. Thank your ancestors. This is your lucky day, the king was going to drive that spear through your numb skull. What do you want?"

"I am only a messenger, isn't it our African tradition that a messenger is never at fault. If I die, I will have died the death of a mouse seeking nothing of substance in a rich man's house. I beg you hear me out."

"Speak, I said."

"It is the way of life that men wrong each other..."

"What do you know about wrongs? The king would have slaughtered all of you by himself, but a man does not start fighting before his ironsmith has forged his spears. Consider yourself lucky, now is not the time for his war."

"Do you know what has been done to us?"

"Not all of it, your highness."

"The yellow bearded man has no respect for us, no consideration, we shall treat him the same when our time comes. He was victorious in his invasion. We accepted that. To the victour goes the spoils. But your yellow beaded men transgressed the land and God's law when they hung the great king from a tree like a cow. It should never have been done. It is better you spear a man's heart to kill him than to string him up. And to add insult to injury before the eyes of the ancestors, they opened his sepulcher as if it was a rabbit hole in the ground. We have all seen this with our own eyes. Just wait and see."

"Your Highness, I had no idea," the *baas boy* said, bowing his head. "Please forgive my ignorance. My words are meant to be peaceful, conciliatory. I come in the shadow of a giant, this young prince of Matonga whom you bore. I ask you to hear me as he has heard me. If I offend you, or the one you speak for, I beg forgiveness before I speak."

He paused, then continued, his voice low.

"I too come from a land that once had its own people. I stand on your soil because I lost my home and the legacy of my ancestors. I have nothing but the employment of the white men who sent me here."

There was silence. But her gaze was sharp, and it held contempt.

"Your Highness," he said again, "I come as a messenger of the white men."

"That much is clear," she replied. "You've drunk from the cup of the enemy."

"The same men who fought the king and now rule over this kingdom did the same to my people. But life goes on, that is its way. Men wrong each other here on earth, and they will continue to do so. Our people say, 'A debt remains a debt, even after the body turns to dust.' I am here because there is a debt that cannot be swept out of sight. My employers may not know its full weight, from the days of war to now, but they know it must be paid. Can we not at least sit and begin to take account?"

"You may take all the accounts you wish," she said coldly. "But I have only one thing for you, a warning."

She cleared her throat, her voice firm and deliberate.

"Stay away from the king's house. Do not go near his grave again. If you do, it will be a personal affront. I swear by my father, the Lion is not one to be trifled with."

She turned from the *baas boy* and faced Chamboko.

"Didn't I tell you to leave?"

"Yes, Your Highness, but…"

"Leave now. This is a war you cannot fight. You pleased the king with your work. Leave while the path is still open. The wrath of the ancestors is blind. Take our prince away."

She rose and picked up the spear and thrust it into the ground.

"Go well, Matonga. You have pleased us all," she said to Edmond. Then she entered the hut, spread the reed mat on the floor, removed her bracelets, and lay down as she had the first time they left.

&

Chamboko offered a few kind words to the *baas boy*, but nothing he said could soften the biting air of anger that vaMatinenga had unleashed. There was nothing more to be done, they had been ordered to leave.

Together, they departed and returned to the mine.

The *baas boy* invited them to stay the night, but Edmond declined. They gathered the bundles they had left in his hut and set off toward Chikwepa's farm.

Edmond no longer feared the dark, nor the wilderness that surrounded them.

They stayed on the wide road. Each day, Chamboko, who had sworn he'd had enough motorcar rides to last a lifetime, found himself praying that no motorcar would come. Edmond, on the other hand, prayed for one. But no motorcar came, and eventually Edmond resigned himself to walking the entire way.

Three weeks later, they arrived back at Chikwepa's farm.

Epilogue

"Behind him lay the world of men; before him, the path the ancestors had chosen."

The five hundred miles back to Chikwepa's farm barely registered in Tarwa's mind; he was too preoccupied. The journey to his fatherland had opened his eyes to the weight of the legacy resting on his shoulders. It had become a rite of passage, a transformation from boy to man, from servant to prince. Though no crown awaited him, he had set foot on his own land, eaten its fruits, and drunk its water.

On their way back, after the spirits had decreed that this was not yet the time for his return to fight and reclaim the lost kingdom, Tarwa and Chamboko had spent the night in the cave where the late king's treasures were kept. At dawn, before their departure, Tarwa had surveyed the treasures with a new sense of ownership. He knew nothing of gold or coins or their worth, nor what he would one day do with them. Yet instinctively, he took a pouch of elephant-hide from the rock shelf and filled it with gold ingots and coins from the broken clay pot on the floor. He considered taking another pouch for Chamboko to carry but dismissed the thought. He would return for the rest in time.

When he finally reached Chikwepa's farm, he felt the difference in his spirit. Unlike Chamboko, who had returned to Matonganyika only to find a land that no longer needed him, leaving his life without purpose: Tarwa had found his place. He had found the purpose of his life. The spirits of his ancestors had sung high praises of the young man he had become. They had placed the future of his clan upon his shoulders. And though he did not know what the future would hold, the burden did not feel heavy. He felt ready.

What would the future bring?
What would become of his relationship with Mr. Jim?
Would he become the son vaMahwata longed for - by becoming his son-in-law?

*How much were the gold and coins in the elephant-hide pouch worth?
And how would that wealth begin the long road toward the recovery of
the lost kingdom of Matonganyika?*

ALF E F MURONDA

Culture, Theatre & Literature - Griot!

Home   About   Books   Contact

www.alfmurondabooks.com

Alf E.F. Muronda is a Zimbabwean-born playwright, poet, and storyteller whose work spans continents and genres. A graduate of UCLA's Theater Arts MFA program, he crafts stage plays, screenplays, novels, and poetry that pulse with ancestral memory, cultural identity, and the human spirit in motion. His published works include *High Class Natives—Ballroom Dancers & Mbira Players*, *Echoes of My African Mind*, *The Role of Drama in the Struggle for South Africa*, *Juliet Mugoti*, *Tarwa*, *Contemporary African Art Abstracted by Valentine Mutasa*, and *Success Thru Goals*.

Whether on the page or the stage, Alf invites audiences to travel between worlds—bridging tradition and modernity with a voice that is both urgent and timeless.

ISBN: 978-1-965398-42-5
© Elfigio F Muronda
Published by MASAKA PUBLISHING MEDIA HOUSE
alf@cp7sisters.com